# MAGGIE'S SONG

# MAGGIE'S SONG

## FULL CIRCLE - BOOK I

BY

# MARCIA WARE

# Dedication

To Grandma, Daddy, Mom, Margaret, Maria and Alan...
where the circle began.

To David, Lily, Andrew and Addison...
where the circle completes.

And to my Savior, who holds us all together.

Family is everything.

# Chapter 1

The tour bus came to a four way stop in the middle of one of those unincorporated rural towns where only the locals knew its name. As Maggie stared out the window, she spied an empty playground, complete with jungle gym, slides, swings and a merry-go-round. That particular scene always made her smile, because it would forever remind her of the day that changed her life.

Cautiously entering the school cafeteria, a 13 year old Mary Margaret West prayed to heaven that no one would notice her. The rain left the students without the option of eating outside; forcing Maggie to find a place in the crowded cafeteria.

*A stranger in a strange land...*

From the day her father packed them up and moved from Chicago to his hometown of Urbana, Ohio, there wasn't a day that passed where Maggie didn't long to return to the city. She missed the days when she could ride her bike three blocks to her Nana's house on Parnell Avenue for cookies that were warm, and hugs that were warmer. It was the only world she had ever known.

But as a young public defender, Dexter West saw the rising crime in the streets, and felt that the best place to raise his only child was in what he perceived to be the more bucolic surroundings of the Buckeye state.

*After all,* he would say, *I grew up there, and I turned out just fine, didn't I?*

Maggie made it a point to never audibly answer that question.

While her mother Lenore didn't mind the move, Maggie still found herself aching to be in a place where her sepia skin and brown curls didn't stand out so much. In this room, the difference she felt in this sea of fair haired children was acute and terrifying.

Her heart lifted at the sight of a cluster of black girls she had seen from her neighborhood sitting in a group toward the entrance. Her gait quickened, and with a smile on her face, began to greet them. After sizing her up, however, the judgment was swift and unanimous: Despite their shared ethnicity, Maggie was not welcome there. The rejection stopped her like a brick wall.

After several attempts to assert herself, she gave up and took a solitary spot at the end of a lunch table. It was then that Maggie overheard the chatter from a group of smartly dressed girls who immediately began their assessment of her. The critique ranged from comments about her slightly pudgy frame-a definite thumbs down, according to them-to high praise for the stylish pink sweater and corduroy ensemble that she actually was forced to wear under mandate from her mother.

Pink was the lone bone of contention between Maggie and her mother. Maggie would have sooner died than be caught in the color, which, in this case, was fairly appropriate since she felt like dying at that very moment.

She could hear the girls talk, and with each comment, Maggie wondered how she would survive the year in that horrible place.

"I heard she's from Chicago…the *south side,*" quipped a

prissy, painfully thin redhead; the words "south side" spoken with some degree of perceived authority.

"I'll bet she was in a street gang…like that show on TV," whispered another in tones that were much louder than intended.

"I don't think they wear clothes like that in street gangs," piped another. The course of their conversation and the absurdity of it made Maggie nearly laugh out loud.

Slowly, she felt her confidence build. She reasoned that it was hard to be angry at ignorance.

"Well, isn't that where the drug dealers and the criminals live? On the South Side?" the redhead asked nervously as she toyed with her sandwich.

"Yep, just like here in Urbana-that's where all the wild kids are. Hanging out at Warren's market, always huddled up in the parking lot around their cars…you just know they're always up to *something…*"

"Um…*hello…I* live on the south side of town. Do *I* look like I sell drugs?"

Maggie looked up from the sandwich she was failing to eat and searched to match the voice to the person.

The girl rose from her place at the table and continued to scold them as she made her way to where Maggie was sitting.

"First of all, she's sitting right here. She can hear every word your saying, for cryin' out loud!"

Maggie was somewhat taken aback by the grown up nature of this approaching child, whose combination of ivory skin and rich brown hair made her look more a porcelain doll that had escaped from a store shelf than the apparent leader of a junior high school clique.

"And secondly," she continued in a cool, cultured tone, "you guys have never been to Warren's market in your life, so you have no idea what you're talking about." She chose the seat directly across from Maggie, casually flipping a lock of sable brown hair over a delicate shoulder. The girl then leaned over the table and said, "Sorry about that, Maggie."

Suddenly, Maggie felt an audacity of her own rise from an unknown source inside…she adopted the other girl's demeanor and threw back her shoulders. "That's alright," she said with a smile. "My dad's a lawyer…and he specializes in taking care of girls who like to gossip about other girls."

"What do you mean…'*take care of?*'" asked the redhead. Her fear was punctuated by a slight gulp mid-sentence.

Maggie knew she now had the upper hand. Completely aware a ruse was in play, her champion waited wide-eyed to see what Maggie was planning to say next.

"Well, let's just say that the last girl who tried to mess with me got picked up and sent to a special school…until she was really, really old."

"How old?" they asked in unison.

Maggie looked over both shoulders as if she were about to unveil the secrets of the universe. With her eyes slightly squinted, she whispered: *twenty…FIVE!*

Four jaws dropped collectively as they slowly rose from the lunch table. "Um, well, we need to scoot - got a project I, um we - need to finish before 6th period…we'll see you later…" the redhead said as the girls practically fell over one another trying to escape potential doom.

"Nice to meet you…*Maggie…*" a blonde girl said politely; the last part of Maggie's name pitched upward as if to make sure she was addressing her correctly.

"Nice to meet you too…"

"Wendy…" The girl responded quickly.

"Right. Nice to meet you too, Wendy," Maggie said with a confident smile.

Slowly backing away from the table, the girls exited with polite, slightly nervous expressions.

Maggie and the other girl continued to nod and wave to the group until they were out of sight. Looking back at one another, they instantly burst out laughing.

"I thought they were gonna all pee their pants," said the brown haired girl, barely able to breathe. "Where did you come up with that story? Did that really happen?"

"Well, sort of," Maggie said. "There was this girl who kept bugging me on my way to school when I was younger; she always threatened to stuff me in one of those big trash cans that get parked on the street. I told my dad-who told her dad...she got a butt whoopin' from her dad and a talking-to from mine that pretty much scared her off of me."

"Really? Your dad's that frightening?"

"You have *no* idea."

The laughter continued for a few minutes before Maggie sobered with her brow slightly furrowed. "Wait a minute...how did you know my name?" she asked.

"I live right next door to you, silly. I'm Grace Hammond."

The light of recognition illuminated Maggie's face as she exclaimed, "Oh...wow! Hi."

"Hi," Grace replied.

And a friendship was born.

As it turned out, Grace's father, Matthew Hammond, and Maggie's father, Dexter West, had their own history that extended as far back to their high school football days. Friendly rivals, they even chose opposing schools - Dexter to Ohio State and Matthew to the University of Michigan.

Their wives joked that such behavior helped to "keep the magic alive."

While Maggie was her parent's only child, Grace had an older sister, Gwen, whom she had christened 'Sissy' when she was four years old. The eight-year age gap between the sisters often found Gwen entrenched in her own activities, leaving Grace to develop her own friends and entertainment.

Maggie's arrival was a godsend to Grace. From the moment they met, one was rarely seen without the other close by. Through bad dates and honors classes, school plays and summer vacations, college, marriage and relationships, they were the constants in each other's lives: The spirited, free thinking, artistic Grace, and the introverted, sensitive, poetic Maggie.

It was Grace who first discovered the diamond in the rough that was Maggie's voice. Maggie was humming absentmindedly one afternoon when Grace made her way over for a visit. She waited outside the door, astonished by the beauty of the simple melody.

By the time Maggie realized she had an audience, she recoiled slightly and apologized. "What are you sorry for, silly?" Grace exclaimed. "That was great! Have your parents ever heard you sing?"

"I dunno. I guess."

"Well, do you like to sing? Please say yes, because you've gotta be just about the best singer I've ever heard and it would be a total bummer if you didn't, I mean, like, what a waste!"

Grace seemed to carry on all of her conversations with a rapid fire intensity that Maggie always found amusing. There was rarely time to offer a response when Grace got passionate about a particular cause. And Grace was almost always passionate about something.

"I think you need to get your name in lights, make a record, and let me design all of your album covers - pictures and all! Promise me you will, Maggie! It'll be great!"

Maggie loved the power of Grace's confidence. It made her feel anything was possible.

"Sure, Gracie. You bet."

They were sixteen years old.

# Chapter 2

Hitting the brakes just a little too hard, the bus driver's abrupt motion jarred Maggie from her reverie.

"Sorry 'bout that gang," the bus driver said. "Blown semi tire in the road. Came outta nowhere."

From the back, items could be heard falling from various bunk beds to the floor, followed by several profanities from surprised passengers. It was then Maggie realized a young woman was sitting opposite her trying to get her attention.

"Hellooooo?" the girl said, slowly waving her hands in front of Maggie's face. "Where in the world is Maggie West?"

The question brought Maggie back to the present as she turned her focus to the numbers of people filling up the front lounge of the tour bus. Maggie couldn't help but smile at the young girl's histrionics.

"I'm sorry, Chrissy. Guess I was just deep in thought."

Chrissy Boyd was unfazed as she continued her probe. "Soooo," she cooed, resting her chin on her knuckles…were you thinking about *him?*"

Maggie pulled a brush from her tote and began to smooth out her tangled mane. She stopped brushing just long enough to arch an eyebrow. "Him…him, *who?*"

"The way you were smiling to yourself, I figured you were thinkin' 'bout your man," Chrissy replied, in a slightly coaxing tone. Pint-sized and brunette, all energy and idealism, her twenty-three years sat very close to the surface.

Still in the blush of her honeymoon, Chrissy wanted to see the whole world in love.

"My man," Maggie sighed, putting slight emphasis on both words. "Nope, I wasn't thinking about him."

"Is he coming to pick you up when we get back?"

"Nah, I'm gonna hitch a ride with Darla."

"You didn't *ask* Darla," came a sultry voice from behind a newspaper.

"Beg pardon, your majesty. Might I trouble you for a ride home?" Maggie chided in a mock British accent.

"Yes my child, you may," said the voice, its owner still concealed by the paper.

"Thank you ever so much."

Diametrically opposed to Chrissy's youthful exuberance was the stunning Darla Dayton. Blonde, cool and aloof; she was an industry veteran who managed to mix down home sweetness and Hollywood glamour: a true country music golden girl. Her taut skin and naturally honeyed tresses gave no clue as to her exact age: Her birth certificate was under tighter security than the Hope Diamond.

"So Maggie," Chrissy interrupted, "What's up with you and Mr. GQ these days? You guys any closer to getting married?"

"Not everyone needs to be married, dumplin'," Darla said, still staring at the paper.

"Not everyone needs to be the subject of a Joe Nichols song either."

Chrissy's quick return seemed to get everyone's

attention. The prospect of a cat fight seemed imminent.

Darla finally turned down a corner of her *USA Today*. Peering over rarely-seen reading glasses, she snapped, "He said that wasn't about me."

"Well, you *do* like your tequila, girlfriend," said Chrissy with faux innocence while nonchalantly buffing her nails. Whistles, whoops and laughter filled the bus as Darla threw down the paper and pretended to go for Chrissy's throat. "Oh, I'm gonna get you for that you little…"

"Ladies, *ladies...*" Maggie interrupted. "You realize you're feeding the imaginations of the men on this bus. They're just hoping you get oiled up and duke it out."

"You say that like it's a bad thing, Maggie," commented a man at the front of the lounge as he casually practiced notes on his guitar.

"Yeah," Darla agreed.

Maggie rolled her eyes. Pointing first at the guitar player, she scolded, "Roger, just pay attention to whatever it is you're doing." Turning to Darla she said, "Girl…sit down and read your paper. *Please.*"

Picking it up, Darla pouted, "You're no fun today, lady."

Maggie laughed, "Well, somebody's gotta be the designated grown-up on this thing."

Such were the ways that time was passed on this particular bus. For the past three and a half weeks, this caravan of players, singers, guitar, sound and lighting techs had logged some serious miles across the country…all in the name of their leader - country music's *diva du jour*, Deana Timmons.

A staple in the Nashville scene for over a decade, Deana was on the verge of realizing mainstream success on the pop charts. And for the lion's share of those years,

Maggie was there, helping to write the songs, arrange the harmonies and perfect the sound that would elevate Deana to royalty among her fans as well as her peers and critics.

As an African American in Country music, Maggie wasn't exactly an anomaly; the genre was changing earnestly enough. But Maggie would be the first to admit that she didn't choose this world…it chose her.

Entering without ceremony to the back of a crowded west Nashville club was Deana's husband and road manager, Charles. He made a point to stop by the annual university showcase that featured roughly a half dozen seniors from the local college performing 20 minute sets in the hopes of instant discovery.

That night, it would be Maggie's turn.

By the time she took the stage, Charles was ready to leave, having endured several less than remarkable performers. As his hand reached the frame of the door, he heard that voice. Smooth. Deep. Arresting and soulful. Charles was impressed.

An invitation to the Timmons home was extended, and Maggie was offered a job as a background singer two weeks before her college graduation. It wasn't a record deal, but it was a steady gig - and she was always game for a learning experience.

And a career in music was born.

From the time she came to the city as an eager undergraduate, Maggie had spent much of her time even before entering Deana's world as one of the more sought-after session singers in town. A local favorite in her own right, she sang solo in various clubs around town. Her performances were hailed by the local trades as never to be missed.

She knew when the time was right there would plenty

opportunity to show the world what *she* could do. If it weren't for that nagging sense of time running through the hourglass so quickly…

Standing at the waning edge of her 30's, Maggie's chances for landing that elusive recording contract were, if her boyfriend Richard was to be believed, dwindling by the second. The music industry wasn't exactly clamoring for 30-something women looking to start a career in music.

And then, there was the issue of image. Maggie was a woman of ample figure with curves to spare. There were occasional remarks from industry insiders and well meaning acquaintances that she'd be much more successful in the business if she dropped fifty pounds.

One label representative told her, somewhat bluntly, that he wouldn't sign her because her body wouldn't look good in print or video. "Great voice, kid," he said. "But this business *is what it is.*"

Maggie's personal fears and insecurities relegated her to the dark club stages and the shadows of more aesthetically palatable, albeit far less talented women in the business that *was what it was.*

Over time in the Timmons camp, however, she went from merely being a hired gun to a part of the familial surroundings Charles and Deana worked tirelessly to cultivate among their staff. With no children of their own, they came to view their team as offspring, with the words "Family First" emblazoned on the back of their tour bus.

*Family First* was also the title of Deana's breakthrough album and the song for which she'd best become known. She ended all her shows with it, and many a banner would rise from the sold out audiences with the words etched across anything from old bed sheets to poster board. Eight of the ten songs on that project were either written or co-written by Maggie. She had become Deana's creative right arm.

And on this particular morning, on this particular tour bus, that right arm was tired and ready for a break.

One more show…but not just any show. The Queen was returning to her throne. They were headed home - to Nashville. Then, a much deserved rest.

Back road became highway, which slowly began to reveal to the city's impressive skyline. Maggie smiled. Despite its rich tradition, the cadre of respected musicians and songwriters the city was known for producing, and the burgeoning diversity of styles, the mainstream music industry wonks in LA and New York dismissed Nashville as a poor relation, a b-list community. For Maggie, however, this town would always be her first love. It was the city that cradled her ambitions and nurtured her talents. In her mind, there was no better place to be.

Maggie fished around in her purse to retrieve her cell phone. She vacillated between her desire to call Grace and her obligation to phone Richard. Her relationship with Richard Davidson, a handsome, prominent entertainment lawyer, served more as an appeasement to her father, rather than any real romantic connection. While Dexter felt a certain degree of pride over his daughter's accomplishments, her choice of music over law was an obvious disappointment.

Maggie figured the next best thing to being a lawyer might be to marry one. Not that marriage was something that was on either of their minds.

Maggie decided she'd phone her best friend to let her know that she'd be home in a few hours. Speed dialing the Buchanan residence, the voice mail eventually kicked in.

"Hello, you have reached the Buchanan's."

It was a voice that thrilled Maggie's heart to the core: her goddaughter and namesake, eight year old Mary Margaret, more affectionately known as M&M. The child's endearingly businesslike message continued.

"Momma, Daddy, Gwen, Matty and me can't come to the phone right now - but leave your name and number and we'll call you back. Oh you gotta do it after the beep. Bye!"

"Hey gang, it's Mag. We're just hitting I-65 and we'll be in town right around 5. I'll call you when I get back to the house, but I was hoping to catch you now…because I wanted to let you know I not only have great seats for the show, but I've got those badges to get you backstage…so tell little Gwennie, she's finally gonna get to meet her hero, Deana Timmons! I believe that this officially makes me cool and you two officially lame! Ha ha. Love you guys, can't wait to see you."

Maggie was sure Richard wasn't waiting by the phone to hear from her. There would be plenty of time to contact him later. Her heart was already at the Buchanan's dinner table - the place she felt most at home. Besides, if her suspicions are correct, he'd found his own way of passing the time.

The bus pulled into the parking lot of a local shopping mall, where the band members had left their cars. Departures were swift and jovial, with Maggie and Darla packed up and on their way in a matter of minutes. "That's the beauty of being a singer," Darla quipped. "You always have your equipment packed and ready to roll."

Maggie lived in the quiet, suburban area of Franklin, a town about fifteen minutes south of downtown Nashville. She'd chosen this Rockwellian town for its similarity to her home in Urbana - the centers of both towns were practically identical.

As Darla pulled into the driveway of Maggie's condo, two cars were already parked: One was Maggie's, the other vehicle had an occupant inside, windows rolled shut and a steady bass throbbing from what was obviously music turned up loud. It was Grace.

"Wow," said Darla. "She's definitely trying to drown *something* out. What on earth is she listening to?"

Maggie closed her eyes in concentration. "Duran Duran."

Darla winced. "Really?"

"Yeah. You can take the child out of the 80's…"

"She does know that there has been other music written and recorded since then, right?"

"Not as far as she's concerned."

"Bless her heart," Darla sighed, uttering the ubiquitous phrase of the South.

Maggie knew Darla spoke with more sympathy than sarcasm, and chuckled softly. "Yeah…I'm not sure what's going on, but you're right, something's up."

"Well, good luck, hon. See you tomorrow night. What time's sound check?"

"I'm gonna get there a little early, but we'll kick off at 4:30," Maggie said as the two women embraced. "See you then."

# Chapter 3

Maggie grabbed her things from Darla's trunk and made her way Grace's car. She could see Grace through the tinted windows, head back, eyes shut, and the strains of "Rio" filling the car.

Shaking her head and laughing to herself, Maggie knocked on the window. Remarkably, Grace immediately responded. She simultaneously rolled down the window and turned down the music. "You know, there *is* a noise ordinance," Maggie said sarcastically.

"Sorry officer," Grace countered. The two women laughed as Grace got out of the car to hug her best friend.

"Maggie, I've missed you!" she exclaimed. "How are you?"

"Good. Tired, but good."

Maggie loosened her hold, but Grace held fast. "I knew it…" Maggie said, pulling back, "What's up?"

Grace looked quizzically at her. "Up? What do you mean *up*? Nothing's up."

"Girl, you're in my driveway with Simon LeBon cranked to 11. What's going on?"

Grace was evasive. "Let's get you inside and unpacked. I have a surprise for you for you. You go ahead and I'll get it, Okay?"

Maggie raised a brow. "Ohhhhhh-kay," she said skeptically.

Deciding that getting to the bottom of Grace's mystery

was far more important than unpacking, Maggie took her luggage upstairs to the bedroom and left it in the middle of the floor. She changed into one of her dad's old Ohio State football jerseys and grey sweat pants, and headed to the kitchen to find Grace busying herself with restocking the refrigerator.

"You got me *groceries*? You're a doll! Thank you!" Maggie exclaimed with delight. "Seriously sweetie…you did not have to do this!"

"Oh please! You've been gone for three weeks, and you always live on takeout right before you go so you don't let any food go to waste. I knew your cupboards would be bare, Mother Hubbard!"

"You are the best," said Maggie, joining in on the activity. She mentally wrestled with how to approach what was obviously plaguing Grace, who had a bad habit of avoiding subjects with any available distraction.

"Okay, in my backpack upstairs, I've got your tickets and your meet-and-greet passes to get backstage," Maggie said, opting for the indirect route to the point.

"Hmmm…" Grace responded absent-mindedly, not slowing her work for a second. The efforts weren't lost on Maggie, who simply stopped what she was doing, leaned against the counter top, folded her arms and continued.

"You're gonna love the seats…"

There was no response from Grace. Maggie continued.

"Yeah, it's gonna be so exciting…there will be some serious Nashville celebrity backstage that night. Maybe even some folks from L.A. All the entertainment networks will be there. It's gonna be huge."

"Uh huh. that's nice."

Maggie moved in closer to see if Grace was even aware

of her presence at that point. "And I'm especially psyched because Bert and Ernie are planning to stop by. So is Bugs Bunny. Oscar the Grouch. Generalissimo Franco."

Now practically sitting in the pantry, Grace was silent, and Maggie was getting irritated.

"Grace. Grace?" Maggie placed her hand over Grace's as the latter attempted to organize soup cans. "*Gracie....stop!*" Maggie yelled. "Now what's going on? Come on girl, talk to me."

Grace finally ceased her flurry, stood up and turned around. Facing Maggie she sighed, "Okay. I'm sorry. I'll tell you. But, can we please open a bottle of wine first?"

"Of course," Maggie said softly as she turned to survey the contents of her wine rack. Removing a bottle of vintage Malbec, Grace said, "I noticed that's the one thing in this house I've never needed to replace at grocery time."

"Hey, I'm trapped in a 12-bunk zoo with all manner of musical animals for like, a bazillion years at a time," Maggie cracked as she pulled the cork out of the bottle. "I've earned my alcoholism."

Maggie retrieved the wine and two glasses, and took them into the living room. Gathering her legs underneath her, she settled into the corner of her sectional sofa. "Okay. Start talking."

"Well," said Grace, taking a sip of her wine and placing it on the coffee table. "I guess it's not that big of a deal...okay, it *could* be a big deal...it didn't start out as a big deal, but now it's looking as though it's probably gonna to become one..."

"Do I need to be here for this part of the conversation, Grace?"

"Sorry. So, we're all set to go to your concert tomorrow. Joe's really been looking forward to it; because it means that we're gonna spend time together as a family. We've not had time to do that for a while, because of my work with the Art Center…"

"Yes…"

"Well, at the center, there have been some changes. The grant I'd been working for came through…"

"Oh Gracie, that's great, I know you lobbied hard for that. I'm so proud of you!"

"Thanks. That's the upside. Because it means we can take about half a dozen more kids. Oh, those kids…" As her mind began to drift, her voice took on a far away tone.

"Gracie…" Maggie said, attempting to cut through the fog. "Focus, honey. Please."

"Right. Sorry. So, more kids…coming at a really bad time, because Ronnie's off to have her baby, and Darryl's taking that job in Seattle…"

"So, the rest of the staff needs to pick up the slack for a while."

"Exactly."

"And they're looking to you to pick up more hours."

"Absolutely."

"In addition to the time you're putting in teaching at the Academy."

"Yep."

"And Joe has no clue that this is all to begin…"

"Next week", they say in unison. "Yeah," said Grace. "It all kicks off this Monday morning."

"Oh boy," Maggie sighed. "This *is* what we would call a pretty big deal, sweetie. How long have you known?"

"About a month."

"Grace!"

"I know, I know. "Every time I try to tell him, I just lose

my nerve. He was hoping that the summer Arts program would be minimal."

"Define *minimal.*"

"Oh, maybe 15 to 20 hours a week," Grace said. "Turns out, we're looking at like *60* hours each with all the administrative stuff and fund raising they want me to do in addition to my instruction. They love the way I hustled to get this last grant. They think I'm perfect for the job. And I'll tell you the worst part…"

"Oh, this gets *worse?*"

"The truth of the matter is that I'm feeling guilty…because…"

"…because you don't really feel that guilty?"

It felt so good to have someone understand. Grace half smiled. "Precisely. I realized when that grant came through, that I *am* perfect for the job. They really need me, and I really want it, Mags."

"Do you have a clue what you're going to do next?"

"What I should have done weeks ago."

"Well, you know that Joe's not a tyrant. You're not marching to your death here."

"I know. But you know how he gets when something disappoints him."

"Girl, please. I'm not even married to him and *I* hate letting him down."

"I mean, there was so much I wanted to do between little Gwennie and the twins…but I just didn't want to rock the boat. We've made this great life here, Joe and me, ya know?"

Maggie sympathetically touched Grace's hand as the latter leaned back on a large throw pillow, closed her eyes and exhaled a deep sigh of her own. "I know," Maggie said.

"I just feel like if I tell him what I'm feeling…"

"Grace, give the guy some credit. I mean, I know he cried when he saw *Mr. Holland's Opus,* but the guy's made of stern stuff."

The women laughed. Maggie went on. "Seriously, trust him not to shut down on you."

Grace wiped an emerging tear from her eye. "Yeah, thanks hon."

"Call me tomorrow?"

"I will."

"Oh, wait…"

Maggie made a quick sprint up stairs to her room, returning just as quickly with a large manila envelope containing tickets and back stage laminates.

"You guys won't get too far without these," she said smiling. "Now, I don't have to be downtown until 3:30, so, a call any time before then will be fine, okay?"

"Okay."

"I love you, Gracie. Hey, let me pay you back for those groceries."

"Oh, don't sweat it-You already paid me back by just listening."

A final embrace before Grace made her way back to her car. "I love you too," she said.

# Chapter 4

The Buchanan residence was a sprawling structure on the outskirts of Franklin that dated back to the Civil War. When they bought it shortly before their marriage, the refurbishing became a team effort, with Maggie and both the Hammond and the Buchanan families pitching in to spruce up the place. As it transformed from an ancient ailing farmhouse to spacious living area, it easily became the center of many a holiday and family celebration.

Grace's artistic touch allowed a bit of city style to be added the décor without detracting from the rustic charm of it all. "Comfortably lavish," was the way Maggie always described it.

As she pulled her car into the garage they had built onto the side, Grace summoned all of her courage in one breath and said quietly, "Okay, God. Help me out here."

Joe Buchanan was a picture of academic repose in his study. Grace stood in the doorway and observed this sensitive soul. She chided herself for thinking that this gentle man could send her into a state of panic. This was *Joe.* The love of her life. What on earth was making her so nervous?

When she met him, he was an associate professor of English Literature at the university she and Maggie attended in Nashville. As if scripted from some romantic novel, Joe Buchanan was the object of many an undergraduate fantasy: Dark wavy hair cascading an inch or so below the nape of his neck; a faint hint of facial hair that covered the deep olive skin that was a direct result of Greek ancestry on his mother's side. Initially, Grace found him to be a bit too intense for her taste - she always liked being the one to bring the fire to a relationship.

Passionate about his career, but rather awkward in his social graces, it was rare when Joe would cast his eyes on a young lady in any fashion other than professional. But when 18 year old Grace Hammond became a member of the student population, her porcelain beauty immediately caught his attention.

Even though he knew there was a mutual attraction, acting on anything would be insane. It was a rare occurrence to even see them in anything beyond brief casual conversation. But as they moved in their individual orbits, there was the intermittent sidelong glance that would indicate that there was definitely something growing below the surface.

It was, in fact one of those quick, chance glances where, if either would have hesitated or chosen another line of sight, the final opportunity would have been forever missed. But in that strange way in which worlds collide, at the midpoint of Grace's senior year, she and Joe locked onto one another from across the commons area in the student union. He was checking his office mail, she was chatting over coffee with Maggie.

A nod of the head from her. A shy smile from him.

And a romance was born.

With Joe not wanting to leave the Nashville of his youth, Grace adjusted her New York dreams to build on his. He supported her as she acquired her master's degree. She then supported him through his eventual promotion head of the university's English department.

*We can do this,* she would reason internally. *I can get him out to New York for some romantic getaways...get him to love the city as much as I do. He can teach, I can create. We'll get there. We've got all the time in the world.*

But then little Gwen was born. Three years later, the twins arrived. Gazing down into the cribs of her little miracles, in their shining eyes and sleepy smiles she could see the Manhattan skyline slowly fade from view.

It was one of the few things on which Grace was reluctant to speak. Expressing any disappointment, she'd convinced herself, would more than likely be construed as selfish. Her priorities were different now. This was her life. And while it wasn't bad by any stretch of the imagination, there was always the "I wonder" and the "what if" that lingered in the back of her mind.

To ease the pain somewhat, Grace accepted a teaching position in the art department at an exclusive prep school in Franklin. She was certain she could inject life into its staid, patrician ways. Her efforts, however, were brutally rebuffed at nearly every turn. The conservative methods of the school's century-old traditions would remain intact, as would the general discontent with her life.

Enter the artisans of the Williamson Community Arts Center, more informally referred to as Com/Arts. Each of these children was chosen out of the public school system for their advanced skills in sketching, painting, sculpting and other forms of creative expression. Participation at this after school program had the potential to lead to scholarships to major universities around the world for kids who had the talent, but not the means.

Grace didn't earn a cent for her time; she gave it willingly. But she gave to the point of detraction from her own family. She was drawn to the Com/Arts kids because they were eager to learn and grasped every opportunity to stretch and expand every time they walked through the door. For Grace, it was a dream come true.

At the prep school, the students were innocently caught up in the materialism of the day. They were more concerned with toys and high tech gadgets that doting, privileged parents would lavish upon them by simple request. For these children, art was merely something to get through; the *easy A* many of them assumed they'd get to bolster their grade point averages; merely a stepping stone on the way to the more important subjects of life.

As much as Grace didn't want to admit it, her children were part of the upscale masses. She and Joe tried to raise them with a more down to earth approach to living; a number of the Com/Arts kids who spent many an hour at their home became close to their own kids.

But every once in a while, the outcries for Wiis, I-pads and cell phones with all the features would fill the hallways of the Buchanan household. In her guilt over spending so much time out of the home, she would sometimes relent, quietly resenting herself for her hypocrisy.

She loved her husband. She loved her children. But to her, life was becoming more unrecognizable by the moment.

# Chapter 5

Leaning against the doorway, Grace whispered, "Hey Buddy." He looked up from the papers on his desk and smiled a weary, but delighted smile.

"Angelfish," he said. As always at the sound of her nickname, she felt a small part of herself melt away. *Please don't look at me like that,* she thought. *This is hard enough as it is without you looking at me that way.*

As she entered the room, he rounded his desk to hug her. "Did you get to spend some time with Maggie?" he asked. She'd not told him where she was going to be, but Joe was somewhat aware of Maggie's schedule.

He knew where his wife would be the second her best friend came back to town.

"Yep."

"So how is our songbird?"

"She's a little tired, but good."

"Was *he* at the house?" Joe asked, referencing Richard.

Grace loved how she and Joe were always good for a gossip from time to time. No time like the present.

"No, *he* wasn't there, and I didn't bring him up," she said.

"Do you think they're even still together?"

"Well, they are when it suits him," she said, inspecting some of the day's mail. "But Maggie and I have gone ten or fifteen rounds on that subject, and at this point, she's sticking with the status quo. I dunno…it could be that she's still kowtowing to her dad - he thinks Richard hung the moon…she could be afraid of being on her own…" She paused thoughtfully. "I don't get that situation at all."

"Neither do I. She's such a great person. I mean they look good enough together, I guess, but I think Maggie can do better than him. He does nothing to build her up as a person."

"Tell me about it."

"I mean, she's had those songs she's been writing for ages, but he never encourages her to get out and do her own thing."

"She can sing circles around anyone in this town."

"Exactly," said Joe. "But you wouldn't know it by him. It's as if he doesn't want her to succeed."

Grace stayed in the conversation, even as she opened a bill addressed to her. "You're preachin' to the choir, baby. I mean, it's not for me to tell her how to live her life, but I'd love to give that man a piece of my mind."

Grace was genuinely touched by her husband's sensitivity. "That is so sweet," she purred as she moved in closer to him. "I mean, it's pretty obvious he'd drop you with one punch."

"Nice loyalty, lady," Joe chuckled.

"Well, I mean, come on, the guy has a Bowflex in his office! But I've gotta tell you, I love how you love my best friend."

"Well, she makes it easy," he said, smiling. "She's family."

Grace slipped her arms around Joe's neck, bringing her face close to his in order to kiss him. "You are so wonderful, Buddy," her voice continued in a sultry, sing-songy quality. "Who's got a better hubby than me?"

Arms around her waist, he closed the gap between the two of them. Suddenly, he stopped just short of an actual kiss. "Whoa. Not so fast there, sister. What's going on?"

Grace pouted, "What do you mean?"

"Grace…" he scolded.

She continued to feign ignorance. Attempting to resume their kiss, she said, "What?"

Joe squinted in recognition of the moment. "You little con artist," he said, bouncing an index finger on the tip of her nose. "That's where Matty gets it from. I can't believe I almost let you fool me again. What's going on?"

Grace backed away, hands in the air. "Fine, I give up. Yes, there is something we need to discuss."

Joe ran a hand through his hair before folding his own arms to brace himself. Grace drew in a breath and dove in head first.

"The art center…" she began.

"I figured," he replied.

"Well Bud, I've got some good news and some, *challenging* news," She fumbled nervously with her car keys to the point where Joe had to take them from her hands.

"Okay," he said calmly. "Start from the beginning."

"The good news is that I got that grant…"

"Honey, that's terrific!" Joe said reaching to hug her. Grace, however, held up a finger to stop him. Never taking her eyes off of him, she backed away to give herself some necessary space. Slowly, she sank into one of the room's green suede wingback chairs.

"Thanks, but that's not all. The grant was big enough to not only make improvements on what we have now, but it's also gonna help us take in about four or five more kids in the fall."

"But I thought you were losing Ronnie and that other guy…Derek?"

"Darryl."

"Yeah, him. Darryl. Anyway, I thought that they were leaving."

"They are."

"Gracie," he half-moaned, "Please don't tell me what I think you're about to tell me."

Grace stood up to plead her case, "Now Joe, listen. It won't be for a long period of time, I promise. Just until we can find Darryl's replacement. And Ronnie will be back after maternity leave…"

Joe's look conveyed disbelief, but he let her continue.

"And they really liked the way I hustled to get this latest grant together, so they want me to take a more active role in how funds are raised…and, until someone comes to pick up the slack…keep up with my instruction."

She winced as if she were about to be struck. Not that Joe ever would - he was generally regarded as the kindest and most patient of men. Always even tempered, there was little that ruffled his feathers.

Until now.

The silence was deafening and seemingly eternal. Finally, Joe spoke as he pinched the bridge of his nose. "Grace, what are you doing to us?"

"Excuse me? To us?

"Yes, to us. You and Me. The Kids. You know - *us.*"

Grace was incredulous. "I wasn't under the impression that there was a problem with *us.*"

"You're kidding, right?"

"No, I'm not. I'm up every morning to see our kids off

to the bus stop. I put in a full day at a teaching job you and I both know is a ludicrous waste of time. I put in three hours at the Center..."

"Sometimes four or five..."

"Okay, I'll give you that one, but I'm *still* home in time to have dinner with the kids."

"A dinner that the kids and I usually cook..."

"Crock pot!" Grace countered.

"What?" Joe asked, confused and exasperated.

"I am the one who puts whatever we're eating in the crock pot in the morning so dinner is ready when you want it. You cut open a bag of salad and boil some noodles. That's hardly cooking," she said.

"Okay, fine." Joe conceded.

"So, we have a hot meal waiting for us almost every night. And even though the house isn't always spotless, we've managed to keep things sane *without* the help of a nanny or a housekeeper. So, I'm sorry if I can't be waiting by the door for you wearing my apron with a martini in hand."

"You know that's not what I'm saying, Grace. I know you're there. But sometimes, when you're at the table at dinner, you're not really *there*. You're a million miles away. And as proud as I am for you helping to make the art center what it's become, I think it's come at a pretty serious cost."

"But Joe, you've seen some of these kids. They've got great hearts, and they are so talented. For some of them, we're their only shot at life. Once we opened up their world to the likes of Pollack or Van Gogh, or any of the impressionists - it was like..." She bit her lip as she searched for a way to better express herself. "It's the most amazing high I've ever experienced. You know, for someone who's never done drugs."

Joe chuckled at her lightness in the middle of such a

serious conversation. He wanted to understand.

"Grace..." he tried to reason. Grace, however, was already gone.

"There's this one kid, Tony. He's nine years old. One day he asked me what I thought it would be like if we only had feet to paint with. So, I said, 'Let's find out.' I gave him a huge canvas, and he started just pouring different colors of paint on it, and skating around like he was on ice. He came up with some of the most amazing abstracts you've ever seen! Then there's Marta...the stuff she can sketch...it's like she's some sort of savant. She looks at it once, and boom! Away she goes. I'm telling you, these kids are just so..."

"Grace," Joe said softly, placing his hands on her shoulders. "I hear you. I do. But *our* kids are *just so...* too."

They faced one another while Grace took in the gravity of that last statement. "I know they are, Buddy," she said softly. "And you know I'd give my very blood for them."

"I know that."

"But you've got to understand something. I'd not only *give* my life; I've *already* given up a good deal of my life to this point."

"Hold on. Given up? Wha-?"

The gauntlet had been thrown. There was no turning back now.

"Joe, I love you. But I got married so young. There was so much of life I'd not experienced yet. New York was a dream of mine..."

"*New York*? Is that what this is about?"

"No. Yeah. Sort of. What I'm trying to say is, I've always been someone's *something*. Matt and Janice's daughter. Sissy's little sister. Maggie's artsy friend, so and so's teacher, the Twins' mom…"

"Joe Buchanan's wife," he said quietly.

"Yes. But not just that one thing in particular; *all* of those things. Don't you see? I've finally found that space just for me. I hoped it would be in Manhattan, but since that didn't pan out, I found Com/Arts. At the Center, I'm *me*. I'm Grace. Everyone else falls under MY category…for the first time in my life," she said as a tear came to her eye, "I feel as though *I* matter."

Joe was astonished. "And you've felt this way…?"

"…for as long as I can remember, to tell you the truth. I could handle not opening up that gallery in The West Village. I could handle you not wowing the masses running the English department at NYU. What slowly began to eat away at me was the fact that I couldn't find *me* anywhere in this Franklin, Tennessee existence we've somehow made for ourselves. I just felt completely lost in the shuffle."

"So, I'm confused. To where is all of this leading?"

"Well," Grace said, "I want to quit the Academy. I hate it there. I'm not the Head Mistress's favorite person anyway. Please. I want to resign."

"And that will free you up to do all you want at the Center."

"Yes!" Grace exclaimed. "Oh, I'm so glad you understand, Joe."

Joe's face darkened with visible irritation. "Yeah I understand. But I don't like the feeling I'm getting."

"What do you mean?"

"Grace, you have a family…"

"I *know* I have a family." The momentary relief she felt was quickly replaced by a growing tension.

"Well is there something about us that you just don't

want to get close to? Do you feel like we're not where you want to be anymore?"

"Oh Buddy, of course not, I'm just saying…"

From somewhere within him, Joe felt the desperation mount. "Grace, please tell me I'm wrong when I say how scared I am; scared that we are gonna completely lose you to someone else's children because of some adolescent dream *that you just will not let die!*"

# Chapter 6

The second the words came out of his mouth, he knew he'd live to regret them. The dumbstruck look on Grace's face confirmed his fear.

"Wow," was all she managed to say. She reached out to the back of a chair to steady herself, wishing he'd just gone ahead and hit her.

"Grace, I'm sor-"

The look she gave him signaled a quick recovery that stopped his apology cold.

"Don't," she said, retrieving her purse with one hand and wiping away a tear with the other. She sniffed. "Do not apologize for something you've obviously wanted to say for a long time."

"But that's not what I meant, Angel. I meant I've done my best to support your efforts from the day we got together…"

"You know what?" she interrupted. "I think we should just table this discussion for another time. I'm gonna go look in on the kids, and go to bed. We'll have plenty of family togetherness tomorrow when we go to see Maggie at Deana's show."

Grace turned and slowly ascended the stairs to the children's rooms to say her good nights. Joe was completely deflated. "Grace, please…" he pleaded. "We promised we'd never go to bed angry with each other."

Grace turned in the middle of the staircase. Looking earnestly at her husband, she flipped a lock of hair over a shoulder. "I'm not angry, Joe. Honestly I'm not. I'm just very, very sad. I can't talk anymore tonight, okay?"

Joe mouthed a silent 'okay' as he nodded his head. With a heavy heart he stood in the doorway of his study and watched her ascend the stairs.

They lay back to back in their bed for a while, until Grace finally let Joe take her in his arms and hold her. The gentleness of his embrace moved her to tears; and he let her cry herself to sleep that night. Occasionally, he kissed her on her forehead; but he never spoke a word to her the entire time.

What could he say? His words had already betrayed him. He knew what he meant to convey, but in the heat of the moment he gave into a knee-jerk reaction instead of thinking things through, which was more in tune with his nature. If fear existed before, it was nothing compared to the churning in his stomach at this point. For the first time in his married life, he wrestled with an unfamiliar sensation: the fact that their marriage was rapidly approaching shaky ground, and neither one of them saw it coming.

Joe's eyes adjusted to the greenish-yellow digital numbers of the clock on the nightstand. His alarm was due to go off in five minutes, but the sound of running water was what crept into his consciousness to stir him awake. Grace was showering, after having been up for nearly two hours already.

She'd gone for a run, packed lunch for the kids, put out the cereal and made toast and coffee for breakfast before waking the kids and finally settling in to see about herself.

Joe even noticed a tie and a shirt of his had been laid out over a chair across the room. She left no stone unturned.

Grace might have never taken a narcotic, but it was clear that when she was troubled, she did have a drug of choice: Relentless activity.

On a normal day, Joe might attempt to playfully steal a sensual moment with his wife in the shower. As busy as their lives had become, they had to work their lovemaking in whenever they could.

This would not be one of those days.

The uneasiness in Joe's stomach had yet to abate. Gathering his courage and his bathrobe, he headed downstairs to the kitchen where Gwen was eating her cereal over the sink, Katy Perry's latest album in her headphones.

Joe marveled at how his daughter was a study in constant evolution. Overnight it seemed she'd gone from cherubic toddler to coltish tween; her lithe figure almost identical to her mother's at that age. The same sable brown hair, stretching past the mid-point of her back, was secured with a simple headband that matched the color of her t-shirt.

A casual flip of her hair over the shoulder brought a smile to Joe's face. That was the first time he'd ever noticed that Gwen had picked up her mother's involuntary habit.

"Morning, Daddy," she said with a mouth full of cereal. The head phones never came out of her ears.

It was fairly normal to see the twelve year old blocking out the world around her with music, in part because she loved it and hoped to be a singer, following in her Aunt Maggie's footsteps someday, but mostly because the music provided much needed relief from the nightmare better known to the rest of the world as Matty and M&M.

Older by thirty six minutes, Mary Margaret felt the need to constantly remind her brother of the fact. She somehow managed to ascertain that since it took him so long to get into the world, he was a good deal inferior and needed her constant help and supervision.

Carefree and always ready to be the center of attention, Matty simply enjoyed throwing things at her, ignoring her tutelage and being a general nuisance at any given opportunity.

Constantly embarrassed by them both, Gwen had convinced herself that she was adopted.

After kissing Gwen on top of her head and removing her earphones - a move that drew a look of sharp indignation, Joe sat at the table to address the twins, who were in the midst of their primary form of communication: arguing. It could be over any topic, for any reason, at any time. And while it could definitely mellow for blissfully brief periods, it never truly ended.

"Good morning young ones," he said. "Now, what's going on here?"

"Daddy, Tell him to give it back," said M&M, reaching for an object that Matty seemed determined to keep out of her reach.

"What is it?"

"It's mine!" the twins scream simultaneously.

"I didn't ask *whose* it is, I asked *what* it is, now come on," Joe said. He stood up and managed to grab Matty's wrist to pry loose the item clutched in his grasp

"What is wrong with the two of you? This doesn't belong to either of you! This is *my tie clip*," he said with frustrated emphasis. "You two will find anything to argue about..."

"You just missed, it Daddy," said Gwen, placing her

books in her backpack. "About ten minutes ago, they were actually arguing over the color of cheese."

"You're kidding," Joe said. Gwen raised a brow and shook her head. "He says it's yellowish orange, she says it's orange-yellow."

"It is," they both exclaimed.

"I told you that you should have sold them when they were babies."

The whole scene was too much for Joe. Burying his face in his hands he exclaimed, "Who *are* you people?"

"They are the little bundles of joy with whom God entrusted us, sent straight from heaven to enrich our lives," Grace said exultantly as she swept through the kitchen. "Now *am-scray*, you little gremlins. Outside…before *I* put you up for grabs on e-bay."

Gwen was already halfway to the door. "This family is so dramatic," she said as the screen door slammed.

"That attitude, little missy, will keep you from tonight's concert," Grace teased as Gwen made a hasty return from the garage.

"Oh mom, please. I'm sorry, I *adore* this family," she said with a brightly manufactured smile.

"Who's being dramatic now?" Grace laughed as she reached into a large duffle bag. Pulling out a manila envelope, Grace continued her torture as she slowly pulled out a stack of what looked to be laminated passes.

"Oh my gosh, are we going *backstage?!?*" Gwen shrieked, her voice rising in pitch with each word. "Aunt Maggie's the best! I can't wait to get to school. I'm gonna be the bomb when I tell my friends! Thank you, thank you, thank you, *thank you!*"

Joe looked at his daughter as if she was a foreign object. "And 'the bomb' is something you *wanna* be, right?"

His question was lost in Gwen's euphoria. The twins giggled at the silliness of it all.

"Wow, didn't know that this is what it took to get a little affection from you, sweetie," Grace said as she returned her daughter's embrace. "But you are more than welcome."

Grace and Joe caught one another's eye and exchanged smiles. It was clear that morning brought with it a certain air of relief.

"Are we really gonna see Tina Timmons tonight Mama?" said Matty.

"It's *Deana* Timmons, bucket head," said M&M.

"Shut up!"

"Make me!"

"Alright, *enough!*" Grace said "Please get your book bags and your lunches and take world war three outside now. I'll meet you at the end of the driveway to wait for the bus."

As the children made their way outside, Joe crossed the uncomfortable space to take Grace's hands in his. "Amazing how good the silence feels once *your* children leave the room," she said with a wry smile.

"How do they just magically become *my* children when the act this way?"

"It's just easier the put the blame on you."

They both laughed softly. Knowing something needed to happen; they both began to speak at the same time. "Go ahead," she said.

"You first," said Joe.

"Well, I just wanted to say that I am so sorry the way I ambushed you last night. Not just with the Com/Arts thing, but with the way I was feeling about my life. That was so wrong of me to just totally unload like that."

"It's alright, hon. I understand. You need to talk to me

about this stuff. I hate that it's been building up for so long with you. I'm sorry too. I really didn't mean what I said about the adolescent dream. That was a rash reaction to everything..."

"I know, I know..."

"We both messed up last night. But your dreams, your identity, your life - those things are huge, and I don't want you regretting one single second of any of it. Your happiness is important to me. *You* are important to me. We will work this out, Angelfish, I promise."

"For better, for worse, right?"

"That's what the preacher told me to say."

They sealed their pact with a slow, deep, relaxed kiss. The pace at which they both fell into the emotion of the act reminded them that it had been quite some time since they'd allowed themselves that kind of physical indulgence. Touching foreheads, Joe whispered, "I'm sorry we never got to New York."

"Hey," she said as she moved in to hug him. "Never say never. We've got all the time in the world, Buddy."

"That we do, Angelfish. That we do."

"See you tonight, Bud. I love you."

"I love you too."

The sound of a car's horn cut through the tenderness of their moment like a machete.

"Matty," they said in unison.

"I've got some spare time today," Joe said as Grace gathered her things to head out the door. "I can check and see if you can actually sell a kid on e bay."

Grace gave her husband a shocked expression. "Joe! You shouldn't even joke about a thing like that."

"I was kidding," he said.

"No, I mean...it would only be a matter of time before

someone tried to send him back," she said. Her deadpan expression made Joe laugh out loud.

"God gave us that child for one reason and one reason only," she continued as she shouldered her tote.

"And what, pray tell, is that?"

"No one else could ever dare handle him." Another honk of the horn. She turned her attention toward the garage. "*Matthew Joseph Buchanan*," she yelled, using a loud, guttural tone. "Do we need to have a come-to-Jesus meeting or are you gonna lay off of that horn?"

Joe chuckled to himself as he poured a cup of coffee. Suddenly, he remembered: "Oh honey, before you go; what's the status on Maggie's birthday party?"

Grace momentarily returned her attention back to Joe, slightly distracted by the realization that her son had just *broken into* a locked car to sound the horn.

"Um, I ordered the cake yesterday; it will be delivered Tuesday afternoon. She's supposed come over around 6 for dinner Tuesday night, but she's got no clue that her parents and mine are coming. The twins are in charge of the decorations."

"Oh Lord."

"Yeah, that should be interesting," she laughed. "Gwennie's working on a fantastic homemade card with a poem she's written; Richard's bringing drinks, and you, my love, are in charge, as always, of the grill."

"Sounds great. Looks like its grocery shopping tomorrow, then."

"You got it." Another blast from the car horn. "*I'm coming!*" she screamed as she walked out the door to the open garage.

Grace continued to scold her son as they made their

way to the end of the drive. Joe grabbed his mug of coffee and went to the front of the house to watch his family head off into their day.

"Thank you God," he sighed. "Thank you for that amazing woman. Thank you for the fact that I get to spend the rest of my life with her. Thank you."

# Chapter 7

The atmosphere in the halls of Nashville's Bridgestone Arena was nothing short of electric. Musicians and celebrities from various walks of life came to mix and mingle; an assortment of record executives, managers, assistants, paparazzi, journalists and hangers-on lurked backstage as well. With every single ticket sold, *A Night with Deana* was shaping up to be the event of year to date.

Maggie sat pensively in her dressing room as the sounds of the first of two opening acts began. Between sound checks, rehearsals, errands and final wardrobe fittings, she had little time for more than a quick phone call to Grace to make sure the Buchanans had everything they needed for the night. She hoped they were having a great time, and couldn't wait to meet them afterward to hear their take on it all.

Her thoughts held her captive to the point where she didn't hear the door open, momentarily allowing the din of the hallway to seep in. With a confident stride, Richard Davidson made his way across the room to Maggie's side.

"Baby," he said softly as he bent down to whisper in her ear. She barely moved.

"Maggie - Baby, come on. You've gotta finish getting

ready," he said, snapping his fingers. That was enough to bring her back.

"Sorry. Just getting in the zone, I guess. Hi." Maggie placed her hand on Richard's cheek and kissed him sweetly.

"Hi," he responded with equal ardor. He looked down at his watch. 7:25 pm. "So, what are you wearing tonight?"

Maggie made her way to the clothes rack to assemble her outfits. "Well, Deana wants the black and gold for the opener."

"Yeah, you'll look great in that."

"Oh, thank you sweetie…"

"Black always slims you down."

Maggie raised an eyebrow and ignored the backhanded compliment. She went on. "Then a quick change to the sequined gowns for the Motown tribute."

"She's doin' a Motown Tribute?" Richard chuckled grimly. "Gimme a break."

"Richard, please don't start."

Richard drew in a breath and took a moment to admire himself in the mirror. Standing well over six feet tall; his mahogany skin had a flawless, almost velvet appearance to it. Knowing that a night such as this didn't necessarily call for a suit and tie, his fashion A-game would still remain solid. He opted for his casual best: A navy blazer over a classic white cotton shirt and crisp jeans with some Ferragamo boots he thought would fit the occasion. He couldn't bring himself to actually purchase anything close to cowboy boots, but he knew he'd clothed his athletic physique impeccably and appropriately from head to toe.

"Fine," he said, never taking his eyes off of his image. "You go live your little country life with your little country friends; do your twangy, watered-down version *our people's* music and I'll catch up with you back here after the show."

Maggie bowed her head for a moment. She loved what she did, and she loved the people with whom she worked. This was a big night for everyone, not just Deana; and she wasn't about to let Richard take that from her.

"Well, since you can't even remotely wish me well tonight," she said wearily, "why don't you go out to the hall right now and see who you know? As you said, I need to get ready."

He was never sure why he continued to play such cruel and silly games with her. It had to be the high he seemed to get off of the push and pull of their relationship. He was her weakness; never protesting his actions to the point of leaving. The fact that she was willing to take his abuse merely seemed to fuel his fire.

When they met at a fund raiser put on by Deana's label, Star Records, it was a wonderful time; Richard did and said everything right. He was the ideal catch.

Simultaneously charming her father by working in an approved profession, completely bewitching her mother with a subtle magnetism - all while sweeping her off of her own two feet, Maggie thought he was a small piece of heaven sent straight down to earth. There was nothing she wouldn't do for him. Which made it easier for Richard when he discovered that Maggie was one of the most connected women in town.

She, however, never saw herself in that vein. The people she knew happened to be people of influence in an industry she loved. She saw them as her friends and strong acquaintances, not as opportunities or stepping stones.

But Richard did. And it annoyed him that she never

took advantage of what was obviously a fertile professional playground.

Since he knew she was the reason his client list was extensive, he always doled out a little sugar with his vinegar. He didn't want to completely push her away. He always had to give just a little bit to reel her back in. "I'm just teasing, baby," he said, smooth as silk, making his way across the room to her. "I'll wish you good luck, but what would be the point? You know you're gonna be great, and you're gonna look stunning. You always do."

He slid his hands down Maggie's arms, and met her expression in her mirror. Smiling brilliantly, Richard savored the effect his one-two punch had on her. He was working it to the best of his ability. Working it, he hoped, potentially, to the bedroom that night.

In private, he loved her 'extra padding' as he put it. When around others however, it was a bit of an embarrassment to him.

Richard wanted to love her. Maggie was sweet enough to love. But he needed more - or in the realm of the physical, he needed *less*. She was just going to have to do until someone more suitable came along.

As for Maggie, the only reason she seemed to soldier on was that nagging question in the back of her mind: *If not Richard, then who on earth would want me?*

Another gentle kiss on the lips brought a smile to her face. "Thank you, honey. I appreciate that. Now go!" she teased.

"So…you and me later?" he asked.

"Baby, you know the Buchanans are here tonight. We're gonna grab a late bite with them after the show."

Richard tilted his head toward the ceiling, rolled his eyes and let out a groan.

"You don't have to come, you know."

An evening with the Buchanans and their boring, bourgeois suburbanness was something akin to the pleasure of a root canal for Richard. But if enduring that could lead to a night of scratching his itch with Maggie, then so be it.

"Just call me on the cell when the show's over and I'll meet you guys wherever." That would give him just enough time to make more interesting plans.

"What, you're not even gonna sit with them? I got you a seat out there."

"Now, you know I've never sat through one of that woman's shows, and I won't start tonight. Besides, the heads of those two independent labels are here, and I heard in the breeze one of them was looking for counsel."

"You're talking about Simon Ballentine? I told you I'd introduce you after…"

"Maggie," He said, heading toward the door, "you've got enough on your plate. I can say hello on my own."

He did, however, fully intended to drop Maggie's name, just to play it safe.

"Okay, that's great. Do your thing. Now go! We're down to like 30 minutes here."

"Okay, okay," he said. Darla opened the door just as he reached for the knob. He paused to regard the dress Maggie held in her hand. "You know," he said, "the black panels on the side of that dress you're putting on really are gonna bring those hips down. That'll be great!"

Thinking his comments would be taken as encouragement, Richard blew an embarrassed Maggie a kiss, gave a perfunctory acknowledgement to Darla, then left.

Maggie took that moment to duck behind a partition to change. Even out of eyesight, she could feel Darla's disdain. "Do not say a word, Darla. Please? Just don't."

Darla took a seat in front of a mirror and proceeded to check herself over. "I didn't say anything. But if I were going to…"

Just then, Chrissy opened the door and peeked inside. "Is it okay to bring Frank in here?" she asked with her usual cheerfulness.

"Sure, I'm dressed," Maggie said. "Come on in guys."

Frank Boyd towered a good twelve inches over his bride. A comic pair not only in appearance, they were in temperament as well: Frank was so laid back and taciturn, one could actually forget that he was in the room. But he loved his wife, adored her spunk. He kept her grounded and peaceful. They were perfectly suited for one another.

"How's it goin' guys?" Darla asked the couple as Frank took a chair by the door. Chrissy gave herself a last minute check in the mirror. "We're great! Rarin' to go," she said. Frank simply smiled and nodded.

"Hey Frank," Darla teased with an over-emphasized twang, "Watch yourself tonight, ya hear? No swingin' from the chandelier or nothin' you wild thang."

Frank folded his arms and laughed quietly. "I'll try to contain myself, Darla."

With all three singers dressed and coiffed within an inch of their lives, it was time for their pre-concert ritual. Maggie grabbed the other girls' hands and began to sing, *"When peace like a river, attendeth my way. When sorrows like sea billows roll. What e'er be my lot, Thou hast taught me to say…"*

*"It is well…"* the three voices joined in perfect three part harmony. Just then another voice lilted over theirs. Maggie knew that voice. They opened up the circle for Deana to join, and let The Boss Lady take over.

*"It is well, with my soul..."*

Glamorously adorned in gold silk, Deana's burnished chestnut hair was radiant against it. With her voice strong and confident, they completed the hymn.

"Girls, are you excited tonight," she asked with a wide grin.

"Absolutely!" they all said, attempting to match her enthusiasm.

"Have a great show. Whoo! I am *nervous!*" Deana twisted and turned to view various angles of herself; fussing with her outfit and her hair anxiously.

"Seriously?" Chrissy asked.

"Oh yeah," Deana explained. "This is the home crowd. You know - a prophet in his own country and all that." She chatted nervously as she flailed her arms wildly for emphasis.

Darla rolled her eyes while Maggie gave her a look of warning; simultaneously placing her hand on Deana's shoulder. "It's gonna be great, Deana," Maggie said reassuringly.

"Oh yeah, I know it is," Deana said, trying to center herself. "I have the best band, the best singers, and the best material in the entire world."

"Does that mean we're getting a raise?" Darla asked. Maggie gave Darla a light tap on the back of the head. "Shut up, D," she said out of the side of her mouth.

Maggie had worked in this business long enough to know that Deana and Charles would change her personnel on a whim for any or no reason at all. Darla had worked in the business long enough not to care.

Darla was fortunate in this case, as Deana heard nothing; oblivious to anything other than the next seventy-five minutes of her life. With an eagerness that could only denote emotions bordering on terror, she said, "Alright! Let's go bring the house down!"

Frank opened the door, allowing the ladies to make their exit. Darla grabbed Maggie's hand, pulled her close and said, "Hey, it was a prime moment to squeeze some more cash out of her. Strike while the mood is good, know what I'm sayin'?"

"Darla, you're a trip," said Maggie laughing.

As the band took the stage, the lights went down, sending the already energetic crowd into a state of near hysteria. The show got underway and sailed without a glitch.

Back in the dressing room, buried in the pocket of her handbag, Maggie's cell phone began to ring.

# Chapter 8

Grace looked at her car's dashboard clock as she put the key in the ignition: 6:15 pm. She was going to be just a little late, but she didn't care about the opening acts. All she wanted was to see Maggie take the stage with Deana Timmons.

By a sheer miracle, Ronnie Parker, whose maternity leave was supposed to start that day, had managed to recruit a number of Art Education majors from the university to come to the center and supervise the children in exchange for academic credit. That allowed Grace a chance to leave early to join her family. "My gift to you, sweetie," Ronnie told her.

Grace lost no time in getting home and cleaning up. Joe and the kids had no idea she was going to be able to meet them for most of the show, and she couldn't wait to call and tell them that she was on the way. She'd not felt this exhilarated in quite some time.

Joe was pulling into a space in the parking garage when his cell phone began to ring.

"Hey Buddy," Grace exclaimed.

"Hey Angelfish," he said. "We just got to the arena. We'll keep a look out for you."

"Well, you won't have to be on watch too long; I'm about 15 minutes behind you."

"You're kidding!" Joe put his hand over the phone to speak to the children. "Hey guys, this is your mom…"

"We know," said Matty, dejected. "She's gonna be late."

"Shows you what you know, mister, she's gonna meet us here in about 15 minutes." The kids squealed with excitement. "Did you hear that?" Joe asked.

"Sure did," Grace said as she pulled up to a stop light. She figured that a Friday night on the Interstate would slow her down with the combination of concert attendees and downtown night life traffic that was in abundance during this time of year. She opted for the consistent flow of Franklin Road instead. "I heard 'em loud and clear."

"Alright now, get off of the phone. You know I hate it when you try to talk and drive."

"Yeah, yeah, yeah," she said teasingly as the green light gave her permission to move ahead.

There was little time to even see the ragged, weathered Camaro speeding from Harding Place at Grace's left into the intersection. There was little time for the drunken teen behind the wheel to react to the fact that there was a red light for him, and an SUV taking her right of way through the space.

# Chapter 9

The sound Joe heard from Grace's cell phone just before the signal dropped was harsh and deafening. Unsure exactly what it was, a sickening feeling began to develop within him.

*"Grace?"*

Confused and nervous, Joe tried not to fear the worst as he shuttled his kids against the building. "What's wrong, Daddy?" asked M&M.

"Um, nothing, honey," Joe said. "I think something's wrong with Mommy's phone. Gwennie, watch the kids."

Joe stepped away from the children and hit the speed dial button on his phone. The brief relief he felt at the sound of the call being taken quickly dissipated when the voice that answered did not belong to Grace. Rather, it was a man with a slow Tennessee drawl. "Um hello?"

Suppressing his emotion, Joe spoke as calmly as he possibly could. "Who is this?"

"I'm sorry sir, who is *this?*" came the response. It was more than Joe could take.

"*This* is the husband of the woman who owns that phone. I know this, because I hit the speed dial on my phone to get her. Now will you kindly tell me what you're doing on Grace Buchanan's phone?" Despite his low volume, the intensity of his speech was the same as if he were shouting.

The twins were busy chatting and singing to themselves, but Gwen watched her father's body language closely. She knew that something wasn't right.

"Mr. Buchanan?" the voice asked. "I'm sorry, Mr. Buchanan, but I was witness to an accident. There was a woman driving a dark blue sport utility vehicle right there in front of me. This old muscle car came outta nowhere and hit her pretty hard…"

After the description of his wife's vehicle, comprehension was difficult for Joe. He heard the man's voice; he knew there was an explanation being given. But the crowd of people excitedly making their way into the arena made the din excruciating.

*Why is everything so loud?* He thought. *Could everything just...please...quiet...down? I can't think... Grace... Oh please... Help us please God...*

"…and I wouldn't have even realized there was a phone if you hadn't called. I was running to get to the crash, and actually almost stepped on it. It was just laying there on the side of the road like nothing ever happened to it…" the voice continued on.

"Okay, just tell me," Joe said between short breaths, "Where is my wife? Can she come to the phone?"

"Well, I'm gonna let you talk to this officer here," the man said as he called a police officer to his side. Barely intelligible conversation followed as the disembodied voice gave instruction to what seemed to be the officer in question. The friendly drawl was then replaced by a more authoritative tone.

"Am I speaking with Mr. Buchanan?"

"Yeah, this is Joe Buchanan," Joe said as he started

directing the kids back toward their car. Matty began to protest, but Gwen put a finger to her lips to silence him and mouthed, "Get in the car."

A glance between Joe and his eldest daughter signaled to him that she knew something was going on, even if she wasn't sure what. He handed her the keys. "Listen to the radio, okay?" He instructed the three of them. Miraculously, they obeyed without struggle.

"Sorry, officer. My wife. Grace Buchanan. I know it's her - it's a blue Ford Escape with a bumper sticker from our kid's school on the back right fender, right?"

That information, combined with the check they'd already run on the license plate was enough to convince the officer to give Joe more information. "Mr. Buchanan, this is Officer Kent of the Nashville PD. I'm afraid all that I can tell you is that your wife has been in a two car collision where she was broadsided by another individual."

"Why can't I speak with her?" He pleaded.

"Sir, I understand your apprehension, but we're taking her to Vanderbilt right now. I suggest you get there as soon as you can."

# Chapter 10

Joe pinched the bridge of his nose, drew in a deep breath, then got into the car, where two blissfully unaware 10 year olds were singing along to the latest Deana Timmons single on the radio. Gwen never took her eyes off of her father the entire time.

"Is Mom okay, Daddy?" she asked as he sat down.

"Yeah Dad. Why aren't we going inside?" asked Mary Margaret. Joe faced his three children with all the reserve he could muster.

"Well, it looks like someone bumped their car into Mom's and she got hurt, so we're gonna go see about her at the hospital." His news was met with slight confusion and concern. "Hey, don't worry guys, we're gonna go see her. She's gonna be fine, okay?"

As the car left the garage and made its way toward the hospital, the mood inside was somber and silent. Suddenly, Matty piped, "Hey Dad. Shouldn't we call Aunt Maggie to let her know where we are? I mean, since we're probably gonna be late for the concert?"

The boy's concern touched Joe deeply. Fighting tears, he pulled out his cell phone and handed it to Matty.

"You do the honors, kiddo," Joe said, smiling into the rear view mirror. Matty dialed Aunt Maggie's number from memory, just like his mother had taught him.

# Chapter 11

The concert was a night of entertainment that would not be equaled in Music City for quite some time. The press would hail Deana's songs as some of the most innovative and groundbreaking of her career. Maggie's name would gain greater buzz throughout the city for her role in giving the music its brilliance.

Still high from the energy of the evening, Maggie and Darla entered Maggie's dressing room, exuberant. "Girl, you nailed those ad libs on 'How Do You Love,'" Darla exclaimed, flopping down into a padded chair. "You were amazing."

"*We* were amazing," Maggie said breathlessly. "I just love how this band clicks; it was awesome. Hey, did you see Grace and her family wandering around back stage?"

"Nope, sorry," Darla said.

"Let me call this girl and find out where they are," Maggie said as she searched for her phone. She noticed there were two calls she'd missed. "Oh, Joe called," she said, slightly surprised. "Knowing Grace, she got here in time for the last song."

As Maggie listened to her godson's voice mail, followed by an update from Joe, her smile became a clouded expression. She started gathering her belongings in a hectic and unorganized fashion.

"Maggie?" Darla asked.

"Um, I've gotta go. That was Joe. Grace has been in a car accident."

"Oh, I'm so sorry," Darla said. "Is it bad?"

Maggie stopped momentarily. "It isn't good, I'm afraid. But Joe couldn't tell me much. I've gotta get out of here. If you see Richard, tell him…"

"Honey, I'll take care of the other stuff, and bring it by your house. Don't worry about this; don't worry about Richard. I've gotcha covered. Go!" said Darla.

As soon as Maggie rounded the corner from the emergency room's entrance the children spotted her and immediately made their way toward her. She reached out to hug the twins tightly as they clung to her and cried. "It's gonna be okay, guys," she said softly. "It's all gonna be okay."

By the time she reached Maggie, Gwen finally allowed herself to really cry for the first time that evening. "Aunt Maggie, I'm so scared!"

"I know, honey, I know. Where's your dad?"

Gwen pointed to a solitary figure, hunched in a chair, head in hands. Maggie led the children back to their father. "Joe? It's me, Maggie. I'm here."

He raised his head to meet her gaze. He smiled weakly past his fatigue and fear.

"I'm sorry I'm just now getting here - I only got your message when the concert ended…"

"The show…" he said. "Maggie, I'm so sor-"

"Are you insane?" she broke in. "Don't worry about it. Just tell me what's going on. Where is she?"

Joe rose to his feet, ran his hands through his hair and exhaled sharply. "Well, all we know so far is that when she came in, she was unconscious and banged up pretty bad, but that's about it. I've told the kids that no news is good news."

The low volume of his voice barely concealed his emotions. "The kids are scared enough as it is. But the doctor promised he'd be down as soon as he had an update for us."

"Who's been called besides me?" she asked.

"I called Matt and Janice," he said, referring to Grace's parents. "And I just called my mom right before you got here."

The energy Joe expended to keep it all together broke Maggie's heart. She took his hand and said gently, "Okay, let's find a doctor so we can get a better handle on things."

As if her statement conjured him out of thin air, Maggie and Joe turned to see a tall, attractive African American man in medical scrubs make his way toward them.

"Mr. Buchanan?" the man asked. Joe responded with a nod. "I'm Dr. Byrd, part of the team that's taking care of your wife."

"How is she?" asked Maggie.

The doctor gave her a pleased, yet curious look. "Are you family?" he asked.

"She is," Joe interjected. "Please…what's going on with my wife?"

"The team is still working on her. There was some pretty extensive damage. We've had to remove her spleen; and it looks like she's got a crushed pelvis. Both legs and an arm are broken."

"Aw no," Joe whispered. Maggie took his hand again. Dr. Byrd continued.

"I've got to tell you, on the upside, she's holding her

own. Her pressure's remained stable, which is a miracle in and of itself. That's the best I can tell you for now. Our primary objective is to get her through this surgery. After that, we can give you a more accurate picture."

Joe reached out to shake the doctor's hand, muttering a hoarse, "Thank you, Doctor."

"Yes, thank you," echoed Maggie. Dr. Byrd turned to her.

"You're quite welcome," he said. Somewhat sidetracked, the doctor's silence made for a rather awkward moment. "Yes, well…" he said, clearing his throat. "Um, I'll be…heading upstairs."

"Thank you again, Doctor," said Maggie, oblivious to the fact that she'd just been the object of a mild flirtation. She turned to Joe. "Well, we'll take whatever good news we can, right?

"Mmm hmmm," Joe said, giving her a mischievous smile.

"What?"

"I'm tellin' your boyfriend," Joe said in a sing-songy fashion as he nudged her with his shoulder.

"What?"

"Flirting."

"I was not flirting, Joe!"

"Not you, silly…him."

"Oh he was not!"

"Was so," Joe argued playfully.

Maggie raised an eyebrow and returned the nudge. "Whatever. You're a nut. Anyway, it's just good to hear you laugh."

Joe put his arm around Maggie as the two sat quietly, lifting silent prayers as the life of the hospital emergency room teemed around them. They were both startled by the sound of Maggie's cell phone. The caller ID indicated that it was her father.

"Daddy…hi."

"Baby girl, Matt just called us. How's Grace?"

"She's in surgery. They're saying she's a fighter, but she's banged up really bad. I'm so scared. I wish you guys were here."

"Well, that's why I'm calling. I wanted you to know that your mom and I are on our way with Matt and Janice, so hang tight, okay? Where's her sister?"

It was just then Maggie realized the one person who hadn't been called was Sissy. As her eyes met Joe's, he read Maggie's thoughts instantly. "I'm calling her now," Joe mouthed silently.

✠

Sissy Hammond was dividing her attention between some important contractual paperwork and reheated pork lo mein; her considerably long legs folded one over the other as she studied her work intently.

A member of the Artist and Repertoire department of Star Records for over a decade, Sissy decided to strike out on her own when the Nashville headquarters opened shop in Los Angeles. Her success afforded her a modest house in the hills - while still a spacious showplace by anyone's standards; it was dwarfed in comparison to the various celebrities and moguls who populated the area. Still, it had the modern charm and opulence she felt was fitting for a woman of her station in the entertainment industry.

A life that allowed little room for socializing beyond the string of gatherings, album releases and post-award show parties, Sissy was comfortably - though not altogether contentedly-living the fast paced single life. There were men who crossed her path, some relationships that had promise, but ultimately none that took root.

But if she could design for herself the perfect companion, it would be Joe Buchanan. She often teased her baby sister for snagging "the last great guy in her age group." There was definitely a large grain of truth in much Sissy's teasing. With Joe being only a year older than her, it was difficult for Sissy to not be slightly envious of Grace.

She picked up her phone halfway through the second ring. "Gwen Hammond." Her focus was still on the task in front of her. "Sissy" was a hometown nickname by which few on the coast knew her.

"Um, Sissy? Hey, it's Joe." That was enough to capture the whole of her attention. She swallowed the food she'd just lifted into her mouth quickly.

"Hey there, Joe! Wow, it's great to hear from you…what's up?"

Joe's voice was shaky and low. "Sis, listen, Grace is in the hospital. There was an accident…and it's bad…"

As Joe apprised her of the situation, Sissy was already headed to her bedroom to pack a bag.

"I'm getting the first flight in that I can," was her response. "Tell everyone I'll be there as soon as I can."

"Thanks Sissy. I'll see you. Just pray, okay? Alright…bye."

Their calls ending at roughly the same time, Maggie looked to Joe. "She's on her way," he said with a great deal of heaviness.

"Ma and Daddy are coming in with the Hammonds, too," Maggie replied.

Joe gave in to a sudden surge of frustration. "How long has it been since that doctor was here?"

"I know it feels like forever, but it's only been a few minutes, sweetie. Do you want to sit down?"

*"I can't sit!"* Joe snapped. Maggie blinked in brief surprise, followed by a look of understanding.

Joe was immediately repentant. "Mags, I'm sorry…"

"It's okay," she said. "We're all on pins and needles. It is an understandable response."

The once quiet hallway now resounded with the quick *tap, tap, tap* of rapidly approaching heels.

"Joseph? Joseph…I'm here, darling…

Joe and Maggie turned to see the elegant, petite figure of Elise Buchanan make her way toward them.

"Mom," Joe said with a great deal of relief. "I'm so glad you're here."

"Well of course. So, how's our girl?" She asked in her clipped, direct tone.

"She's in surgery, holding her own," said Joe as he bent down to receive a kiss from her. Elise then turned her attention to Maggie, giving her a kiss on both sides of her face. "Maggie sweetheart, I'm so glad you're here," she said.

"Mom, would it be possible for you to take the kids with you until we know more?" Joe asked.

"Absolutely. Alright you little monkeys," she said to them cheerfully. "How do you feel about coming home with me for a bit, huh?"

The twins cheered. To them, a day at Gramma's Belle Meade mansion was better than any amusement park. Gwen, however, was reticent. "Daddy?" she said to Joe.

"Go ahead, hon - help your Gramma," He reached out to hug her. "Everything's gonna be fine. Okay?"

Gwen smiled weakly and looked up into his eyes. "Okay."

As Elise skirted the children away, Gwen stole a glance back to Joe and Maggie. Their smiles may have been meant to reassure her, but they were trying to reassure themselves as well.

The doctors worked on Grace throughout the night. As dawn approached, they were cautiously optimistic, listing Grace in stable, but serious condition. It would be hours however, before they would have a more accurate picture of her prognosis.

After what seemed like an eternity, Joe and Maggie were finally allowed to sit with Grace. Her tiny frame was lost in a mass of equipment, wires and bandages; it took both Joe and Maggie a few seconds to recover from the shock of what they saw.

Joe creased his brow in anguish, choking back tears at the sight of her. Rounding the bed to her left side, they saw the most visible damage of the impact. As if her face had been evenly divided, the entire left side was an accumulation of cuts and bruises, while the other half was barely scathed. Her hair had been shaved to tend to a major head laceration; a large white piece of circular gauze covered the wound. Her neck was stabilized by a white foam collar. The swelling of her cheek was evidence of a fracture.

Joe pushed a chair as close as he could to that side of Grace's bed. Tentatively, he put a hand on top of hers and stroked it softly. A nurse entered the room for a routine monitoring. "Go ahead and talk to her," she said to Joe. "She can hear you."

But Joe said nothing. He simply put his head down next to her.

Maggie chose that moment to make a quiet exit to check on everyone's arrival. She first phoned her parents. Reaching her mother, she found out that their original flight was canceled due to mechanical problems, but they were put on another flight that was getting ready to depart at that moment. She could only assume that Sissy was en route as her calls went straight to voice mail. Somewhere in the flurry of activity Richard had called to check on Grace's progress.

Managing to actually sound sincere, he promised to be there as soon as he could, but that was the least of Maggie's concerns.

Wearily, she made her way back to Grace's room. Joe remained face down at the side of the bed. He was breathing steadily, leading Maggie to believe that he'd drifted off to sleep. She crept quietly to the bedside, staring intently into Grace's face, as if somehow she could rearrange the jumbled mess of skin and bones into a familiar picture.

Kissing her own fingertips, Maggie moved them to touch Grace's forehead, then the top of Joe's head, lifting up a prayer for both of them. She curled up on a worn leather couch in the room, silently watching her friends until her eyelids could no longer stay open.

# Chapter 12

Maggie and Joe were awakened at the same time by a page requesting the immediate presence of a doctor somewhere on the floor. Through bleary eyes, they smiled and said, "Good morning," to one another.

"It's morning?" came another voice. It was hoarse, slightly slurred, and mostly mumbled. But it was definitely a voice. And it was definitely coming from Grace.

Maggie nearly tripped over her own feet as she crossed the room. Joe rose slowly and cautiously. "Hey there, Angelfish," he said softly.

"Hi honey," Maggie chimed as she made her way to the opposite side. "Good to see you."

"Good to be seen," Grace whispered. "Wha- what happened? I'm not dead, am I?"

Maggie closed her eyes and inhaled, smiling. "Oh sweetie, you had an accident. But the docs fixed you up, and you're gonna be fine."

"Mmm…" was all she could manage to reply. After taking in a breath, she finally spoke.

"Joe?"

"Yes baby?"

"I just need to see your face," she said softly.

He leaned into her field of vision and smiled.

"Here I am."

"Honey, I'm so sorry..." she began

"Hey now," he broke in. "This was not your fault. The cops said that you got broadsided by someone who ran a red light. But like Maggie said, you're gonna be fine." He stroked the loose hair on her uninjured side. "You're gonna be just fine."

For the next few minutes, Joe and Grace engaged in quiet, precious conversation. He poured his heart out to her; she responded in kind as best she could. Maggie felt compelled to allow them that time alone.

Soon, a nurse came into the room. Pleased that Grace was awake, she cheerfully checked her vitals. She then called for Dr. Byrd.

Byrd arrived with a handful of colleagues to look over this seeming miracle. A brief history of the accident was recounted, medical terms and procedures were bandied about, probing questions and answers filled the room. Grace found the intense scrutiny amusing. "Boy," she said quietly. "I'll...do *anything* to...be the center of attention... won't I?"

Everyone in the room laughed.

Because she was funny.

Because she was alive.

With every second that passed, a greater sense of relief and confidence began to grow in the room.

After the examination, Dr. Byrd considered his words thoughtfully. "Well, she made it through the night. That's fantastic. Let's stay on the side of vigilance everyone, okay? I'll be back to check on her in a bit."

The doctors made their exits as Maggie's phone rang. It was Matthew Hammond.

"Maggie, how is she?"

"Awake," Maggie replied. "And yes, she's being a little pistol, as you could well imagine," she continued.

Matt laughed in relief. "Oh, can I ever. Thanks for the good news. I can wait till we get there to hear the rest. I don't want to tie you up. I just wanted you to know our flight was in. I tried to call Joe, but I couldn't get through."

"Joe, check your phone. The folks are here," Maggie said. "Their flight just landed."

"Aw man," he said. "The battery's dead. Tell them I'm on my way to get them right now."

"Joe, I don't think that's such a great idea," Maggie said, her hand over the receiver.

Pausing for a moment to consider what to do, he made a snap decision. "Don't worry," he said. "I'll not be gone long. You stay with her. You heard the doctor. I'll be right back. He made a waving motion requesting Maggie's phone. Reluctantly she gave it to him.

"Hey Dad? Yeah, it's Joe. Listen. Hang tight. I'll meet you at Ground Transportation. It will take you too long to rent a car. We can do that later. I'll be right there."

Maggie felt uneasiness over this arrangement, but she quickly dismissed it for the sake of peace in the room. "Okay Joe. But hurry back."

"Of course."

With an air of exuberance, Joe slowed down just enough to gently kiss Grace. "Your folks are here, honey. I'm gonna go get them. I'll be right back, k?"

"Joe…" she mumbled.

"Relax, Angel. I promise I be just a couple of minutes. Thanks Maggie," he said, handing her back her phone as he sprinted out of the room.

Maggie put on her best game face and made her way

to Grace's bedside. "How're you holding up, sweetie?"

"Oh, I've had better days," she joked. Her smile fading, Grace sobered quickly. "To be honest, I'm a little scared, Mags."

Maggie took her hand. It was rare for Grace to express fear on any level. That, added to Joe's impetuous departure, weighed heavily on Maggie. Instinctively, she knew what to do.

Returning to her cell phone, she found Elise Buchanan's number. She used the hospital phone to make the call.

"Hey Gramma, its Maggie."

"I was just getting ready to call. How is she?"

"Well, hang on…"

Maggie put the receiver to Grace's good ear. "Hey Mom…"

"Grace! Oh honey…Thank Heaven; it's so good to hear your voice! I'm not gonna tire you out, but hang on…Gwen! Get your brother and sister," she called out away from the phone. "I've got a big surprise for you."

As Grace rallied to talk to each of her kids briefly, Maggie marveled at the mercy of God.

Equally concerned about expending Grace's energy, Maggie took over the conversation. Elise offered to bring the children to see her later that morning.

"Okay, Kiddo," Maggie said as she closed the hospital room door, "I think we've had enough excitement for one hour, huh?"

"Mmmm," Grace said.

"Want some water, sweetie?"

"Uh uh," Grace whispered. "Come here. I…want… talk…"

"Gracie, you really need to rest…"

"Maggie…" Grace said through labored breaths. "Please."

Maggie carefully sat next to the bed on her good side and took her hand. "Okay, okay, sweetie. What's on your mind?"

"Listen, Mags. I…love you." Grace said slowly. "I'm…gonna…need…you to…ta-take…care of…things."

"Oh honey, you know I'll always be here for you. And Sissy's on her way…"

"No!" Grace interrupted. "I need… need… it to… be… you. Take…care…of…things…love you…"

Grace's eyes began to flutter shut.

"Gracie…? *Grace?*"

Somewhere in the room, the steady mechanical beeping began a long sustained sound.

Maggie raced to the door.

"I need a doctor in here *NOW!*"

# Chapter 13

Charging to 300...*Clear!*"
The doctors' and nurses' movements were swift and certain, working feverishly to revive Grace from her arrested state.

"Nothing...she's still asystole..."

"Charge it again..." called out one doctor.

"Clear!" said another.

The *thump* of the defibrillator was instantly followed by the metallic sound of Grace's body rising from and returning to her bed.

*"Charge it again!"*

Maggie stood in the hallway, terrified and helpless. Calling Joe was useless; his phone battery was gone. She tried to see what was happening in the room, but to no avail. All she could do was stand outside and listen.

"How long has she been down?" Dr. Byrd asked as he began manual CPR.

"Going on 40 minutes..."

"Dear God," Maggie said as her hand went to her mouth. "Please, don't stop." She prayed. "God, please don't let them stop!"

"No change," said a nurse in a firm, collected tone.

"Keep going - charge to 360," she heard a doctor say.

*"Clear!"*

Joe rounded the corner, with the Hammonds and the

Wests in tow. Almost immediately, their euphoria dimmed to confusion at the sight of Maggie in the hallway.

"What happened?" Joe called out, running to her.

"I don't know, I don't know!" Maggie cried. "One minute we were talking… I was trying to get her to rest… but she insisted…"

Joe tried to enter the room, but was escorted out by a nurse. "Please, Mr. Buchanan, let the doctors work, okay?"

Completely frustrated, Joe walked back to his in-laws, who embraced him. A cell phone rang. It was Sissy, calling her father.

"Dad?"

"Sissy…where are you?"

"I'm just getting to the hospital now. How is she? What's going on?"

"Oh honey, I didn't know when your flight was getting in, or we would have waited for you…just get here as soon as you can. It's room 1109."

"Dad. How is Grace?"

"Sissy, please. Just get here as soon as you can, okay honey?"

Joe tried to enter Grace's room a second time. This time, he didn't come out. Maggie followed him; after that, the Hammonds and the Wests.

Dr. Byrd had his hand on Joe's shoulder, explaining what had happened and what his team did in an attempt to bring her back. Despite their best efforts, her heart could not be revived. Grace Elizabeth Hammond Buchanan was pronounced dead at 9:06 am.

✠

For the longest time, Joe simply stared at the doctor. His face held no expression. The only sound that registered within him was the sound of his own heart beating.

He couldn't hear the anguished sobs of his mother in law as she buried her head in Lenore West's shoulder. Nor could he hear the sounds of machines being turned off and hospital personnel leaving the room.

He never heard Sissy arrive; her long hair whipping around her face at her sudden halt in the doorway.

His whole world had collapsed at the point of the crash's impact, but the dizzying rate at which he was spiraling now was more than he could manage. Dr. Byrd guided him to a nearby chair where he sat, unmoving.

Matthew turned to his eldest daughter and immediately enveloped her in a massive embrace. "Our Gracie's gone," he choked softly. "Gracie's gone."

Her hand to her mouth in shock, silent tears immediately began to spill from her eyes as she broke from her father to make her way to the bedside. "Oh honey," Sissy said as she took Grace's hand, "I'm so sorry...I tried to get here earlier...I tried so hard...I'm sorry, I'm sorry!"

Joe rested his head in his hands, internally berating himself for his reckless behavior.

*I left her. How in the world could I have left her?*

The words tumbled over themselves inside his head to the rhythm of the constant heartbeat that still managed to drown out every external noise. He he was completely unaware that he too was participating in a chorus of wrenching sobs.

# Chapter 14

Dexter offered to rent a minivan and do the driving, giving Joe, Matthew and Janice one less detail to manage. Soon, Joe, the Hammonds, and the Wests all began to prepare themselves for perhaps the most stressful of those details: the viewing of Grace's body.

Directly behind Dexter sat his wife, Lenore; holding one of Janice's hands while Matthew held the other. Maggie was in the back with Sissy. Joe rode silently in the front passenger seat.

Janice was first to break the silence: "I'm so glad you picked that blue crepe suit, Maggie," she said plainly.

"It was her favorite," Maggie said.

"Yes, she always looked so pretty in that shade of blue," Janice continued, hoping desperately that if she continued to talk, it would make the horrific events of the last 48 hours seem as if they'd never happened at all. Reality won out, however, as her sentence trailed at the end to a barely audible tone.

Matthew slipped his left arm around her shoulder, gently rubbing it as he held her close to him. Turning his head away, he looked out the window, uselessly fighting tears of his own.

Baylor McCutcheon made his way out the front door of his

establishment to personally greet the family upon their arrival. Slight, balding and cherubic in appearance, he greeted each family member with an earnestly mournful expression and a warm embrace as he ushered them inside.

"It's so hard to find the right words to say in situations like this…even after all of my years in this business," he said to as he led them to a set of French double doors.

Pausing momentarily with his hand on the doorknob, he took a moment for instruction. "My restorative artist has been working practically 'round the clock in order to be ready for today. Peter's my number one employee in that department, so I hope you'll appreciate his hard work."

In one smooth motion, McCutcheon opened both doors to a tenderly lit room, adorned with dozens of gladiolas and lilies - Grace's favorite flowers. They single-filed down a central aisle between rows of white cushioned folding chairs. At the far end of the room was the casket, with Grace inside. The silver exterior housed a satin lining that was the barest whisper of lavender; made slightly richer by the cobalt blue of Grace's suit. Her lavender blouse was a near exact match to the casket's interior.

As the family moved in closer, they marveled at what they saw. Despite a barely perceptible dot above her left temple, Grace's face was completely free of the snarled mass of cuts and contusions that had invaded her face. A small track of hair had been expertly blended into her own to hide the space that had been shaved and stitched. The sable-brown mass rested gently behind her shoulders, framing the porcelain of her skin. Grace simply looked as though she were sleeping. McCutcheon was right: Peter was the best.

The serene beauty that Grace exuded, even in death, drew quiet sobs from various members of the family.

Maggie continued in stunned silence. When she reached out to touch Grace's hands, a jolting sensation shot from the point of contact, straight up into the center of her own soul.

*So cold...* was Maggie's first thought. The chill she felt was more than just temperature. It was only then that she realized that despite the heaviness in her heart, at no point had she yet shed a tear. It puzzled and bothered her, as if her stoicism were a sort of betrayal.

"Remarkable. Truly remarkable," Matthew said, continuing to be in awe at the sight of his youngest daughter.

"Oh my sweet little girl," Janice echoed in astonishment. She reached down to touch her daughter's face. "All this time I wandered how they were going to make her look like she did before… or even if they could."

"I brought Mr. McCutcheon a picture," Maggie said.

Sissy was a bit surprised that Maggie would take on a task like that for herself "You did?" she asked.

"Yes," Maggie replied. "It just made sense at the time. She was so badly injured; I wanted to make sure they were as accurate as possible, and not just guessing about anything."

Sissy was at a loss at what felt like an intrusion, but Janice and Matthew were genuinely moved by Maggie's gesture. "Thank you, sweetheart," Janice said, never taking her eyes off of Grace. "That makes total sense. It was so good of you to think of that."

"The fewer details you guys had to tackle, the better, I figured," Maggie said. "I want to do whatever I can to help, you know that."

"How 'bout bringing her back?"

The family turned to stare at Joe, who alone had made

no attempt to approach the casket. He remained transfixed by the door. Collectively they walked toward him, in the same cautious manner in which one would move upon a wounded animal.

"Joe…" Maggie began.

"*No!*" he snapped. His response was filled with that uncharacteristic sharpness that had reared its head in the hospital.

Its whip-like intensity caused Maggie to flinch. "Joe, I'm sorry. I didn't mean… I was just trying to…"

"I'm serious Maggie," he said, his eyes all at once narrowing and flashing fire. "You wanna do something to help? I want you to find a way to get her to sit up in that casket and tell us this was all a mistake. I want you to get her to crack one of those lame jokes of hers that always puts us into hysterics!"

His guilt and despair now fully exposed, Joe let go and allowed his heart to completely unravel. Tears sprang hot from his eyes as he pointed a finger at her and hissed, "If you can do that, *then* you'll be helping out, because anything less is *unacceptable!*"

"Joey, please," Janice pleaded. She reached out her hand to him, but he made a hasty retreat to the door. He stopped short, unsure of what to do.

"I'm sorry guys. I'm just…I just… I can't do this. I gotta get out of here."

Before anyone could stop him, Joe pulled back the French doors and bounded out the front door of the funeral home.

He had no idea how he was going to get home, but at that point, as far as he was concerned, he had no home. Grace was gone, and if he could have found a way to join her he would have.

For now, what he needed was a strong drink. Or two. Or ten. Anything to numb him to this nightmare in which he'd found himself.

# Chapter 15

Maggie felt wretched inside. Her tension had less to do with Joe's departure and more to do with the fact that she knew exactly what her father was thinking.

The look she was choosing to ignore screamed volumes; it said she'd gone too far - that it didn't matter how good her intentions were, she had no business doing what should have been done by Grace's family.

Sissy went to the door to try and stop Joe, but he was half way down the street, well out of ear shot. "Let him go, Sis," Matthew said. "He's gonna have to work this out on his own."

"I understand, Dad," said Sissy as she returned to the group. Shooting Maggie her own look of disapproval, Sissy quickly placed the blame of Joe's distress on Maggie's shoulders.

But the thing that neither her father, nor Sissy, nor anyone else for that matter, would probably ever understand was that every move Maggie made to that point was exactly what Grace would have wanted. Maggie knew her best friend instinctively.

When the bad break-ups came, Maggie always had the right thing to say. When parents didn't understand, Grace understood. When there was a need for sisterly advice, or someone to just sit and listen, it was simply second nature for Maggie and Grace to turn to one another.

It was on a joint shopping excursion that Grace's final suit was found. Despite the hectic nature of both their lives, Maggie and Grace's annual sojourn in Atlanta was an event that bordered on the sacred. Nothing and no one was ever allowed to come between them and that weekend. Life as they knew it ceased to exist back home. It was all about the adventure.

From the moment Maggie held up the cobalt wool crepe jacket and skirt for Grace to try on, she was in love with it completely.

Euphoric, she said in her habitually flippant way, "Oh man, I will wear this thing to my grave. It's so gorgeous!"

Maggie knew. Even if the others would try to surmise what they thought Grace's final wishes might be, in her heart of hearts Maggie was divinely destined to be the one to always get it right.

She was the one person in the world who would, as Grace had requested, take care of everything.

Dexter pulled her aside as the Hammonds continued to make final arrangements for the next day's family viewing and the memorial service with McCutcheon. Before he could get a word out, Maggie held up a hand to stop him. "Daddy," she said, "I know you think I've overstepped my bounds here, but trust me on this."

"Maggie," he said sternly. "I know you two were like sisters. But she *has* a family."

"Dexter, you've made yourself clear," said Lenore. Turning to Maggie, she said "Honey, you dad does have a point. We understand your intentions, so all we're asking is that you clear things with people before you start diving in, okay?"

"You're right guys, I'm sorry."

"Why don't we wait in the car and let them finish things up in here," Lenore said as the trio discreetly slipped past the Hammonds and out the door.

Despite the array of friends and relatives that had found their way to Nashville for the time of mourning, Joe somehow managed to slip into the house largely unnoticed. Only Janice's sister Maria noticed his hasty retreat to the bedroom. She started after him, but he ran up the stairs so quickly that she stopped short at the landing, watching him disappear into the darkness of the second floor. She figured it was best to leave him alone.

Once inside, Joe locked his door and dumped the contents of a large brown grocery bag onto the bed. The liquor bottles clinked gently against one another as they landed.

Never one to indulge in alcohol beyond a couple of glasses of wine over dinner, Joe wasn't sure of how much of the bourbon he would be able to consume. But he wanted something strong, and Kentucky Thunder sounded more than potent enough.

He tore into the first bottle with ferocity, sputtering at the power of the liquor as it burned the back of his throat. He took another drink, casting a long look at the bed he and Grace had shared.

It hadn't been touched since her last morning alive: Joe's side had the covers tossed freely as a result of his typical crack-of-dawn exuberance. Grace's area had the indentation of her usual position: curled up on her side, hugging a pillow.

Since Joe was unable to bring himself to fix the bed, much less sleep in it, he chose to take a blanket to the large cream-colored chaise positioned at the far right side of the room. What little sleep he got in the ensuing nights was punctuated by longer periods of wide eyed staring out into space.

The normalcy of it all was too much to bear…and all the invitation he needed to take another drink. The next few swallows seemed much easier to endure. His body began to feel a gentle hum as the alcohol made its way through his system.

His vision somewhat glossed over, he made his way to Grace's closet. At first, he handled the vast array of blouses, suits, slacks and t-shirts gingerly, studying each item, remembering how she looked in each one. Then, piece by piece, he began to pull the clothes from their well-ordered place in the closet. With each shoe, hat, scarf and blazer, his movements became more feverish, tossing things into a haphazard pile behind him. In his growing frenzy, he stumbled, causing him to fall in on a few remaining dresses he used to steady himself.

Drawing in a deep breath against the fabric, the soft, powdery scent of Paloma Picasso filled his senses as his final descent began.

He clung to a collection of sleeves; eyes squeezed shut, mouth open wide, wailing without sound. He ripped the remaining items from their hangers and tossed them on the pile. Staggering back to his bottle, he took another drink. Tears and inebriation completely clouded his eyesight as he started randomly removing the contents of Grace's chest of drawers.

By the time the Hammonds and the Wests returned to the Buchanan home, dozens had stopped by to offer gifts of food, sympathy and condolence.

Joe's absence, while explained and understood, was becoming far too conspicuous to be continually ignored. Occasionally, an attempt to coax him down among the masses was greeted by the odd, slurred expletive; a sharp demand to simply be left alone, and sometimes, just silence.

As she leaned against the entrance to the den, Maggie suppressed her desire to intervene and chose to focus her attention on what was taking place in front of her.

Janice Hammond was sitting on a sofa, in perfect posture with one leg crossed demurely behind the other. She was staring into a cup of tea, doing her best to maintain a conversation with Joe's best friend and colleague, Declan Young.

Maggie took notice of Sissy's strong resemblance to her mother. The shoulder length, strawberry blonde hair Janice once wore was now a smart, closely cropped style with a few streaks of silver throughout: traits most certainly passed down to her eldest child-along with soft green eyes, a full mouth and a smattering of freckles across the bridge of her nose.

Sissy's long, sturdy build was a gift from her father, but in face and feature, no one could deny that she was Janice's child. And while Grace had adopted the delicate carriage of her mother, her dark eyes, ivory skin and perfectly conditioned brunette hair could clearly be traced to the intensely handsome and now completely grey Matthew Hammond.

"Maggie," Janice said, patting the couch cushion next to her. "Come join us."

"Has anyone heard from Joe?" Declan asked.

"Not, really," said Maggie as she took a seat next to Janice. "Unless you wanna count the stuff he shouts through the door." Matthew grimaced at the thought as he took a sip of his drink.

"How are you holding up?" Maggie asked Janice.

"About as well as can be expected, honey," she said

sweetly. "But I'm curious as to how *you* are doing."

"To be honest, I have no earthly idea. I know I'm awake, I know I'm functioning, but I have no clue as to how I'm doing it. Oh, Mom…I miss her so much already."

Janice took Maggie's hand in hers. Early on in their friendship, the girls took to calling each other's elders 'Mom and Dad', 'Grandma and Grandpa.' At that moment, it was a great comfort for Janice to hear. "I miss her too, sweetheart."

After seeing some more of the guests out, Elise joined the family in the den. "He's not still up there, is he?" she said from the doorway.

"Yeah, Gramma, I'm afraid so," said Maggie.

"Alright now, I'm all for giving him some space," Elise continued, a rare hint of fear in her normally crisp tone. "But this is really starting to trouble me. He's always been a sensitive boy, but this doesn't feel right."

The conversation was halted by the presence of three children in the doorway. The adults turned to see Gwen, Matty and Mary Margaret simply standing there. There was no way to tell how much of the conversation they'd heard.

"Is Daddy okay?" Gwen asked. Thinking she was going to have to repeat her earlier act of shielding her siblings from parental tragedy, terror rose in her throat as tears began to well in her eyes.

For Maggie, the children's agony was the last straw. Pausing briefly to take Gwen's face in her hands, she smiled and said, "He will be honey, so don't worry."

Maggie rushed past her mother and father and made her way quickly but cautiously up the staircase into the darkness.

Her father caught her halfway up, as the rest of the

company waited at the landing. "Maggie," Dexter said sternly while grabbing her arm. "This is *not* your business! Don't you remember anything we discussed?"

"Dex, please!" called Lenore from below.

Without showing intentional disrespect, Maggie shook free of her father's hold and faced him squarely. "Of course I do Dad, but this is getting out of hand. And Grace…Joe…the kids…well, they *are* my business. I can't stand by and let him do this. He's hurting himself, and he's hurting them," she said, gesturing to the family below. "I have to try, Dad."

# Chapter 16

Maggie continued up the stairs and drew a deep breath as the rest of the group watched in anticipation. She wasn't sure how she was going to get through to Joe; but somehow she knew she had to.

As Maggie arrived at Joe's bedroom door, she took a moment to survey her surroundings. The second floor was an open foyer that housed the four bedrooms and the main bathroom of the Buchanan family. The bay window at the end of the hall was outfitted with cushions, pillows and silk plants, much like the window in her own home. A flash of her and Grace sharing coffee and conversation there came and went in the light of a street lamp just outside the window.

She whispered to herself, "Okay, here goes."

Three short raps on the door. "Joe?" she called.

Silence. She tried again. "Joey?"

There was a soft noise, followed by a slurred expletive, requesting solitude.

She paused for a moment, turning her gaze to the staircase. She could see a few faces peering around the corner of the landing, including the critical scowl of her father.

She tried again, but was met with the same, slightly louder response from Joe.

Finally, something inside of her exploded. She'd had enough. She knew that Joe was stronger than this. She also knew that Grace would have been incensed at his behavior.

Her desperation and frustration reaching a fever pitch, she began to pound furiously on the door as she shouted, "That's it! Joseph Buchanan, this ends *right now*!"

The pounding continued as she went on, the loss of her reserve surprising even her. But she wasn't giving up.

"Seriously," she yelled, "We're all hurting now - not just you! We lost a sister, a daughter, a best friend...*the kids lost their mother, for crying out loud!* Stop this right now and open this door, or I'm kicking it down...and *I am NOT kidding!*"

Janice turned her head into Matthew's chest while simultaneously drawing the children toward her. As much as she wanted to see Joe downstairs with the family, she wasn't sure about Maggie's well-intentioned attempt at tough love.

Dexter shook his head as Lenore put a hand to her mouth, hoping desperately that Maggie knew what she was doing. For the briefest of moments, not one person took a breath.

All were surprised, however, when they heard the soft clicks of a door unlocking, opening, and then closing again a few seconds later. Joe had granted Maggie entrance.

Maggie was in shock. The normally pristine bedroom was a wreck. Clothes were scattered and piled throughout the room. Opened love letters and cards littered the floor, loose pictures and photo albums were strewn about the bed.

She carefully navigated the obstacle course to the edge of the bed where Joe sat, head in one hand, his bottle of liquor in the other.

"Oh God," he groaned.

"Well...um, calling on God's a good place to start," she said, still in a state of disbelief.

Joe exhaled sharply, giving Maggie more than accurate access to his self-medication. "Wow, that's quite a scent you've acquired for yourself there, buddy," she said as she turned her head away.

She reached out to place a hand on his back as his own hand sank deeper into his hair. "I left her, Maggie," he said, his voice thick with emotion. "How could I have been so stupid?"

"Joe, I don't think what you did was stupid," she said after a thoughtful moment. "In fact, I think it was very brave."

Joe scoffed. "Brave. Yeah, right."

"Seriously, sweetie. What you did was a total act of faith. You *believed* she was out of the woods. We all did. But you actually went on what you believed. That's pretty amazing." She paused to slowly draw in and release her breath. "What I'm about to say is gonna be a bit hard to hear, but I'm gonna say it anyway."

Joe braced himself and turned a bleary gaze toward Maggie as she continued.

"We prayed for Gracie to get healed. I know that. What we are having a hard time getting our arms around is the fact that she *was*."

Joe gave her a troubled expression. "Healed? How can you possibly say she was healed?"

"I know, it sounds crazy, but death is a kind of healing. Not the kind *we* want, obviously - but it *is* a healing. It's the ultimate healing."

"But I didn't get to say..."

"Honey, stop," she said, cutting him off. "Don't go there. You got to say stuff that was so much more important than 'good bye.' I don't know what you were talking about when I left you guys alone in the hospital room, but I know you both well enough to wager that you were doing some serious fence mending."

A look of appreciation washed over Joe's face. Maggie's understanding of the situation amazed him. He returned his gaze to the floor and said, "Yeah. Yeah we did."

"What a great gift, ya know? That's something that most of us would give our blood for - to be able to make sure that everything you need to say gets said to the people you love. None of us knows the day or the exact hour we're gonna die. So what you had the chance to do was really quite enviable."

Joe covered his eyes with his free hand. He knew she had made a valid point. "You're right Mags, you're so right. Thank you."

"And no matter what happens, there is one truth that's more clear than anything you'll ever know."

"What's that?"

"You've got three little people downstairs who need their daddy desperately."

Joe sat completely upright, scrubbed at his face and ran his hands through his hair once more. They smiled in relief before enveloping in a comfortable hug.

Suddenly, Joe pulled away. His smile faded and his face took on a pained expression.

"Maggie?"

"Joe?"

"Ugh…."

"Oh boy…"

It suddenly occurred to Maggie what was about to happen.

Joe was going to be very, very sick.

The two of them raced to the master bathroom; both thankful that it was only a few steps away.

As Joe began retching into the bowl, Maggie rubbed his back and said, "Okay…it's gonna be alright. This is the bad part, but you're gonna get through it."

*Oh Lord, please help us all,* she thought.

# Chapter 17

Matthew opened the bedroom door, and with a great deal of trepidation, he, Janice and Sissy, the Wests and Elise walked inside.

Instead of a chaotic scene, however, they were greeted by the sight of Maggie having straightened up much of Joe's mess, and the sound of a shower running.

"Wow," said Matt. "Is everything okay?"

"Yeah," Maggie replied with a weary smile. "For the most part, he's cool."

"Boy, he sure did some damage," Elise said, wrinkling her nose at the scent that still hung in the air. "It smells like the morning after in here."

Maggie chuckled, "The morning after what, Gramma?"

Elise raised an eyebrow. "Anything, honey. The morning after *anything.*"

"There are still a few folks downstairs, but pretty much everyone else thought it best to go home," Janice said.

Maggie looked back at the closed bathroom door where Joe wasn't so much showering as he was bracing himself against the wall under the running water. "That's probably best," she said. "I don't think he's in any condition to come down and talk to anybody."

"Now hold on, Maggie," Sissy interjected. "I know you

were Grace's best friend, but I think as Joe's *family*, we know what's best for him, and he needs to be surrounded by people who want to comfort him."

The word 'family' was said with a degree of emphasis that resonated with Dexter, but shocked every else in the room as being unduly harsh.

"Sissy!" Janice said.

"Well, he'll have plenty of time for all of that tomorrow," said Elise firmly. She pointed her finger up at Sissy. "And that's coming from his *mother*, who knows him better than anybody."

Sissy was taken aback by Elise's retort and said, "I'm sorry Gramma, all I was saying was…"

"Look, we're all on edge," Elise said. "I've never seen him this low, obviously, but he's a strong boy. He just needs tonight to sleep it off and sort it out."

She then turned her attention to Maggie, touching her on the arm. "You handled it just fine, dear. Don't you worry about a thing."

The apparent taking of Maggie's side by Elise caused Sissy to burn within. Maintaining her composure, however, she turned to the others and said tersely, "Well, I guess that's that then."

"Come on, I think we all just need to go," said Matthew. "Joe's gonna need his rest."

As they all exited, Lenore embraced her daughter. "I love you baby," she said softly.

"Love you back, Ma. You too, Daddy."

All Dexter could manage was a half smile, a nod and a gesture with his arm to lead the ladies out of the room. As to the effectiveness of Maggie's actions that night, the jury was still out as far as he was concerned.

"Maggie, that dress looks great on you!" Grace exclaimed from the doorway of the dressing room.

Around Grace's feet were several shopping bags, over her arm was a garment bag containing the spoils of her part of their Atlanta shopping weekend: a cobalt blue wool suit and a silk blouse, the barest whisper of lavender.

Maggie took in her refection in the three-way mirror. The chiffon of the dress felt like heaven, the darker shade of silver was perfection against her skin. The v-shaped neckline, gathered waist and full, flirty skirt were a true compliment to her shape.

"Look what I found," Grace said to her in her sing-songy voice as she dangled a pair of pewter Armani pintucked leather pumps over Maggie's shoulder. "These will go perfectly!"

"Oh, they are fabulous," Maggie cried happily. "This is so funny. I feel like I'm your dress-up doll or something."

"I prefer to think of you as my ever-evolving canvas," Grace pronounced triumphantly as she sat down in a dressing room chair. She draped her leg over the chair's arm and flipped her hair back over her shoulder.

"And *you* are a work of art, baby," she laughed, pointing at Maggie.

Maggie slipped on the pumps and studied herself more intently. "It all works, doesn't it?"

"Of course it does, honey," Grace responded in dramatic fashion, hands flung high in the air. "Every woman deserves to be, at one point in her life or another, swathed from shoulder to sole in anything from Alexander McQueen to Zac Posen. If you don't buy it, I'm buying it for you."

*...I'm buying it for you... buying it for you... for you...*

The words echoed in Maggie's head as her eyes slowly opened to the dawn.

Glancing at the clock, she realized that in two hours, a host of friends, family and colleagues would gather to remember Grace in tribute. In roughly three hours, Grace's body would go to its final resting place.

For a few moments, however, Maggie decided lay curled up with a pillow, replaying what she could remember of her dreams of Grace over in her mind.

When she finally decided to rise, Maggie went straight to the closet and pulled out the same beautiful designer dress and matching shoes. She'd never worn the dress before, and after the service, she knew she'd never wear it again. There were no plans to throw it out or give it away. She figured she'd just place it, along with the shoes, in her closet back in the vinyl garment bag from which they came; their significance relevant to no one but her.

Matthew and Declan decided to try and help Joe get ready for the service. Armed with strong black coffee, a large bottle of water and some vitamin B, Matthew still found it difficult to wake him. The relief of getting sick and the hot shower afterward had a soporific effect on him, causing him to fall into a deep sleep.

"Come on son, it's time to get up" Matthew said. Joe stirred a bit, his eyes not opening.

"Joe? You need to get up now."

Joe let out a groan and put his hand over his eyes. "Ten more minutes. Please," he mumbled.

"I'll keep an eye on him," Declan said. "You go on ahead, Mr. Hammond. I'll get him there."

Matthew placed the coffee mug on the nightstand next to the bed. "Thanks," he said, shaking Declan's hand. "He's gonna need all the support he can get today."

# Chapter 18

It was the church where Joe and Grace were married. But today, there was a much more somber air at New Song Christian Fellowship in Brentwood, as family and friends came to pay their final respects to Grace. If one were to go by the appearance of the sanctuary, it would be a fair assumption that there was not a single lily or gladiola left in the Mid South.

That was her mother's doing: she wanted to make sure that there were plenty of Grace's favorite flowers surrounding her one last time.

The stories told about Grace were bittersweet - lots of laughter through tears. The children of Com/Arts created banners and pictures that were displayed on easels throughout the room. Students from the music department at the academy where she taught sang hymns in her honor.

Twenty minutes into the service, Joe still had yet to arrive. Matthew kept one eye on the events in front of him, and one eye on the door. The pastor was about to take the podium to give the eulogy. After that, Maggie would sing, and it would be time to go to the cemetery. *Oh Lord,* Matthew prayed. *Please don't let Joe miss this. Please get him here safely. He will never forgive himself if doesn't make it.*

Maggie rose slowly from her seat and made her way to the piano. Placing a hand on it to steady herself, she turned and faced the congregation. "When I first moved to Ohio with my family, I never knew that right next door was a living, breathing force of nature. But that was Grace."

Soft laughter and affirmation from the audience signaled agreement.

"She was the sister I never had. There isn't one thing about my life she didn't know. She believed in me…not just my music, but in me as a person. There was never judgment - but plenty of advice, though…heavens! The girl had an opinion about *everything*, didn't she?"

The laughter was louder this time. A few responses could be heard throughout. Maggie continued.

"She was the keeper of my secrets, cheerleader for my dreams, the teller of bad jokes…*really* bad jokes. Jokes so bad they were fantastic."

Maggie took her place at the keyboard as friends and family murmured to one another their acknowledgements.

"But the thing I loved most, was no matter how big a fan she was of my music, you just couldn't get that child out of the 80's!"

More laughter as Maggie began to play softly. "Now, I wracked my brain trying to think of which song she'd love to hear today if she was here. I settled on this song by one of the few bands we both loved. In fact, one of my best memories was when we saw this band in concert during our senior year at University."

Closing her eyes, she began playing a song by the pop band Mr. Mister. "The Border" wasn't a well known hit by the band, and that was the way Grace and Maggie liked it. Many an afternoon they spent listening to and enjoying the B-sides of their records as much as the hits they thought were played to death on the radio.

As was her habit, Maggie took the melody and

eventually made it completely her own, giving it color and expression that would give anyone who didn't know the song the impression that she'd written it herself.

Halfway through the second verse, Joe and Declan appeared at the doorway. Slowly, they took their walk down the center aisle of the church. The crowd began to murmur at his approach. Quickly, he quelled the din by gratefully motioning for everyone to continue to pay attention to Maggie as she sang about unanswered questions.

By the time he made it to the front row with the rest of the family, Maggie began her build to an emotional crescendo. She poured every ounce of her energy into the song. Every tear she hadn't wept until that point, every emotion she thought she was yet to express, it went into her song.

Out of respect for Joe's late arrival, the casket was left open during the service. As he arrived at its edge, he reached out to touch Grace on the cheek. The sweetness of Joe saying his last good bye, combined with the power of Maggie's song, left no dry eye in the entire building. And through it all, Grace was there, observing the proceedings with the One who created her. She smiled. "That was amazing," she said to Him. "Thanks for letting me see."

"Well, I did create you to enjoy a good party," He said, smiling.

"They're gonna be fine, aren't they?"

"Of course they are. No need to worry…and no more dawdling. It's time for you to go."

Taking one last look at the scene below, Grace blew a final kiss goodbye to her old world, and embraced her new one.

Family and friends returned at the Buchanan home for a meal and memories. The services now complete, everyone was about the business of celebrating Grace's life. Despite the sadness, there was an air of positive expression throughout.

Joe, still a bit groggy but slowly coming back to life, made up for his disappearance the night before by speaking with as many people as he possibly could.

Surprising everyone, the twins took turns comforting one another; going so far as to spend time looking at vacation videos in the family room. Each appearance of their mother on screen would evoke memories that ranged from the comic to the touching for both of them. Sissy, Gwen and Janice poured over tomes of photo albums in the living room. Dexter and Richard and Lenore carried on a conversation by the fireplace in the den, while Janice's sister Maria handled refreshments from the kitchen.

Maggie watched it all from her place on a couch with a quiet smile. Grace would have gotten a kick out of the whole scene.

As the day wound down and the guests took their leave, the clean up began. Janice took freshly laundered table linens back to the upstairs closet, and stopped for a moment to look in on Joe and Grace's room.

She smiled as she admired her daughter's skill in decoration. The room was still a tad cluttered from the night before, but the beauty was still there, still easily seen.

Instinctively, Janice began picking up the random pieces of clothing, letters and photos that remained out of place. Putting some items in the drawer of Grace's nightstand, Janice noticed something had fallen behind it. She reached down and retrieved a small gold gift bag with a card attached to it that simply said, "Maggie."

"Special Delivery for Miss Maggie West," Janice said sweetly upon her return to the living room.

Suddenly Lenore drew in a gasp of realization. "Oh my goodness," she exclaimed, putting a hand to her cheek. "I cannot believe we forgot!"

As understanding slowly washed over the group, a chorus of "Happy Birthdays" came from various ones in the room. "I'm so sorry," said Lenore. "But, with everything that's happened…"

"Trust me, it was the last thing on my mind too," Maggie said.

"Well," Joe said as he recalled the conversation he and Grace shared on the subject, "It seems a little strange to talk about now, but the timing on this couldn't be more perfect. We'd all planned this massive surprise party for you tonight. Your birthday cake got delivered about 30 minutes ago. Hey gang," he said to the kids. "Go get your stuff for Aunt Maggie's party."

"Joe, we can't have a party now," Maggie objected as the kids scampered up the stairs.

"Of course we can," said Matthew.

"I think Grace would want you to go ahead and do it, Maggie," Sissy said. Her mea culpa was glaringly obvious, but everyone thought it best to let it go.

"Thanks Sis," Maggie said. "Well fine then," she said, clasping her hands together, "Let's um…have some cake."

"Not yet!" said the twins and Gwen as they dashed down the stairs, arms full of the items they'd collected for the party. Maggie was given a tiara, a scepter and a sash with letters boldly spelling "Birthday Princess" on it. Everyone began to chuckle.

"How cute!" someone said. Someone else took out

their cell phone and snapped a picture. "There's one for Facebook," said Declan.

The laughter was light and good natured until Richard said, "Oh, this is too much."

Maggie swore she detected more mocking in his tone than genuine amusement. Her only response to him was a raised eyebrow and a sharp look. She'd deal with him later, she decided. The present moment was all about going with the flow.

"Here you are, sweetheart," said Janice, handing her the gold gift bag. Maggie gave her a questioning look, to which Janice immediately responded "I wish I could take credit for it, but I can't. I found it behind a night stand in Joe and Grace's - um, I mean, the master bedroom."

Sensing her discomfort, Joe tried to lighten things by teasing his mother in law. "Were you rooting around in my things, ma'am?"

"I'm sorry, I didn't mean to snoop," Janice said meekly. "I just saw a few things out of place in your room and wanted to help straighten up a bit. It's a habit of mine, you know."

"She can't live if she sees even the tiniest thing out of order," Matthew interjected.

"Forgive me, Joe. I hope you don't mind."

Joe gave her a gentle squeeze. "Oh, I'll let it go this time." Turning his attention to Maggie, he said, "Let's see what's in the bag."

Maggie pulled a small gold box out of the gift bag. Almost immediately, her heart began to pound. She knew exactly what it was. And she knew exactly from whom it came.

Over the years, Grace had cultivated a talent for, among other things, creating jewelry. She loved making things for family and friends whenever she got a moment.

When it came to Maggie, however, plans were top secret: Grace would go into seclusion and sketch designs months in advance to make intricate, one-of-a-kind pieces just in time for Maggie's birthday.

And it would never go into Maggie's hands until Grace was certain it resembled something that actually could be purchased in an upscale boutique somewhere. Nothing could ever look homemade. With Grace, perfection was the only standard. And no matter where Maggie went, the jewelry always draw raves. Sometimes, when she knew she could get away with it, Maggie would say that she regularly commissioned a top artisan to make the pieces exclusively for her.

It wasn't a total lie…just something about which she and Grace could have a laugh in private.

Of course there were always other gifts, but the jewelry was something Grace did for Maggie without fail. It was her show of sisterhood; a loving tradition.

A tradition that was now over.

There would be no more earrings or bracelets, rings or necklaces. No more shopping weekends. No more late night phone calls, coffee dates, lunches or vacations.

It was all over, never to return. Maggie's hands began to shake as the revelation hit her:

Grace was eternal.

Her face became ashen, her eyes welled with tears. The box and the delicate marcasite pear-shaped earrings inside it fell from her hands into her lap.

"Maggie?" said Lenore. "What's wrong?"

"I - I can't breathe." She absent-mindedly pulled at the tiara and the sash as her eyes created a waterfall.

# Chapter 19

omebody, please help me. I seriously…cannot…
breathe," Maggie whispered. Her words came out in a
short, labored staccato. She tried to stand, but lost her
footing and collapsed on the couch.

"Maggie, sweetheart," said Dexter, kneeling in front of
her, "Come on now, just try and calm down. What is it?"

And finally, Maggie wrapped her arms around herself,
bowed her head, and poured out her soul. The anguish was
deep, bringing the entire house to a standstill.

"Oh, God, help me please! Grace. *Gracie.* Oh, this hurts.
This…hurts…so…*bad!*"

Maggie hadn't able to explain her behavior over the
past few days. Her inability to register significant emotion
both confused and annoyed her. She knew what she felt,
but the ache in her heart and the emotion of the loss were
walled up behind a huge dam, unable to break, no matter
how hard she tried.

But the wall was necessary, because Maggie was, at
Grace's insistence, the one who was meant to take care of
things. She needed the emotional fortitude to carry out
what needed to be done. To hold hands, to soothe hearts,
to encourage decisions that needed to be made in the way
she knew that Grace would approve.

All things completed, it was now her turn to mourn.

Lenore went to her daughter's side and gathered her in her arms. Maggie's sobs were muffled in her mother's shoulder. Dexter moved to the opposite side, trying to understand and simply held her hand. Unsure what to do, Richard thought it best to back away from the action, and retreated to a nearby doorway.

Joe, however, sprang into action, kneeling in front of her as he motioned for Declan.

"Deck, Let's get her upstairs."

In one smooth action, the two men got Maggie to her feet and directly into Declan's arms. As her parents followed after her, Richard took that moment to offer his aid. Placing his arm around Lenore, he said, "No, Mrs. West, they've got her. She'll be alright. Come over here and sit back down. Mr. West, both of you…sit over here." He led them back over to the sofa. "Let me get you some water. You both look as though *you're* gonna faint where you stand."

"Thank you son," Dexter said. "Yes, please get Mrs. West some water."

Richard strode into the kitchen. Filling two glasses with ice and water, he congratulated himself on his quick thinking and returned to the living room.

Joe led Declan to a bonus room that was a short flight of stairs off of the second floor. As Declan placed a still-sobbing Maggie on the bed, Joe calmly encouraged her to take a sedative.

The three Buchanan children tended to her; putting cool washcloths on her head that she most likely never felt. They read her stories and poems and sang songs that she most likely never heard. But they didn't care. Their Aunt

Maggie was hurting, and they weren't about to leave her side.

"Is she alright?" Lenore asked Joe as he returned downstairs.

"Yeah, we gave her something to help her sleep," Joe said.

"She's got three little nursemaids tending to her right now," said Declan said to everyone in the room.

Sitting next to Lenore with his arm around her, Richard said with a concerned expression, "I can't imagine what kind of rest she's gotten up to this point." Alternating between patting and rubbing Lenore's upper arm, he said, "With everything she's been through, she must be exhausted. Thanks for taking care of her. I'll check on her in a few after those kids come down."

Joe nodded, and stayed silent. The way Richard referred to his children as "those kids" didn't pass unnoticed.

"Yeah," Joe said. "Just let her rest here, and we'll make sure she's okay."

Dexter and Lenore looked pensive. "I'm not sure I feel comfortable just leaving her," Lenore said.

Dexter added, "I realize that there's not much more that can be done, but…"

Janice walked up to her friends and grasped their hands gently. She gave the Wests a knowing, compassionate smile. "Maggie has done so much for everyone, you guys. I think it's time for everyone to do something for Maggie. So, don't worry," she said as only one parent could to another. "We know what to do. We've had her with us on sleepovers before."

Janice's light hearted comment sweetly broke the tension as everyone began to laugh. The memory of the two young girls' never-ending slumber parties was bittersweet.

"Okay, Jan. But if she wakes up, tell her we'll be here very first thing tomorrow, please?" Dexter asked.

"Absolutely," said Matthew. "Now go get some rest."

Maggie awoke with a start. She tried to rub her eyes, but found that she couldn't move. As she adjusted to the diffuse light of dawn, she realized that Matty had nestled himself in to her right side with his head on her inner arm. Gwen was on her left, one arm circled around Maggie's waist. Mary Margaret was just below Gwen, holding on to Maggie's legs. All three children had fallen fast asleep at some point during the night.

She was deeply moved by their devotion. Suppressing laughter, she freed herself from their hold, peeling them off one at a time.

Richard had never checked on Maggie as he said he would. He decided that Maggie was in good hands and figured his time would be best spent with the Wests later in the evening.

Maggie knew nothing of his justifications, and would have been surprised if he actually had stayed.

Smoothing herself out as she slowly descended the stairs, she could see that Matt and Janice were in Gwen's bedroom, and Declan had taken up residence on a sofa in the living room; his long legs just hanging off the edge. Maggie gave him a look of pity. Even in sleep, he looked rather uncomfortable. She figured she'd probably robbed him of the only bed in the house that was able to accommodate his exceedingly tall frame.

She detected the smell of fresh coffee coming from the

kitchen. She knew only one person who could be awake that early.

Joe sipped thoughtfully from his mug as he watched the sunrise from his favorite place in the house.

The glassed-in addition was the last thing that he and Grace had decorated together. She designed it to be his personal sanctuary, complete with beanbag, leather and papasan chairs, high school trophies, Tennessee sports memorabilia, and a wide screen television tucked into a far corner. Both would recall that project as being one of the best summers of their lives - because they did it together.

"Is it safe for a lady to enter the man-cave?" Maggie asked as she poked her head through the sliding glass doorway.

Joe gave her a warm smile. "Of course it is, come on in."

He slid over to allow Maggie room on the sofa. Hair slightly tousled, he was still in his dress shirt, slacks and socks. There was a softness to his look that suggested that he'd not been to bed at all.

He offered her his coffee mug and she accepted, taking a sip.

"Ugh", she said feigning choking. "You want a little coffee with this cream and sugar?"

"Oh, that's right," he said slyly. "I forgot how you take your coffee."

Maggie gave him a pointed look. "Oh please, just hush."

Their shared laughter subsided into a lingering silence as they reflected on events of the last few days. There was no discomfort in the quiet, only peaceful recollection.

"Joe," Maggie said finally. "I'm so sorry for losing it like that. I don't know what happened."

"I do," he said, simultaneously turning toward her and slipping his arm around the back of the sofa. "You pushed it all down to keep us all together."

"But that was such an embarrassing display."

"No. It was honest. Real. No one blames you at all. How else could we have gotten through the past week? Please, my abuse alone earned you the right to cry."

Maggie began to refute him, but Joe interrupted her. "No, now I'm serious. I said some ugly things to you. To everyone. Stuff I would have never said to in my right mind. Since I wasn't in any position to be the rock, you stepped up. In fact, I'm gonna use a word you used for me…you were *brave*, Maggie."

Maggie chuckled as her words came back to her. "This conversation does have a rather familiar ring to it," she said.

"You lost, for all intents and purposes, your sister. But you did what you had to do to help the rest of us make it through. And when it was all over, you took your turn to grieve. He casually gave her shoulder a squeeze. "Nothing to be ashamed of, kiddo," he said.

She'd been staring down into the mug of coffee that was now beginning to grow cold. Raising her head, her tear-brimmed eyes met his and she simply said, "Okay."

There were no words left.

He pulled his lips to her forehead and gave her a warm, chaste kiss. "It's time to get us both a fresh cup," said as he took the mug from her hands.

# Chapter 20

Maggie stretched and took in the beauty of the morning that was expanding outside the enclosure. She'd always asserted that when Tennessee was in full verdant bloom, there were few places on earth that were lovelier.

Looking down at her feet, she saw something less lovely: she was in desperate need of a pedicure. The dichotomy was amusing, and she chuckled at the irony.

As Joe returned with two fresh mugs of coffee, he asked "What are you thinking about?"

"Oh, a couple of things," she said softly. "After the folks go home, I know it's gonna be difficult to get your bearings. Whatever it is that you need - I don't care what it is or when you need it, I want you guys to call me."

"Thanks. I'll hold you to that promise. As much as I don't want to admit it, I know I'm gonna need the help."

"Well consider it done."

"I appreciate that. But you said you were thinking about a *couple* of things. What was the other?"

She grinned sheepishly. "I know it's only like six in the morning…but that birthday cake has yet to be eaten, and I gotta tell you, a piece of that with this coffee sounds really good right now."

Joe laughed and rose from the sofa. Extending his

hand to help Maggie up, he said "Okay, but let's make it fast. I hear some stirring upstairs, and the last thing I want to do is hop those kids up on straight sugar first thing in the morning."

"Ooh, I hear that." Maggie quickly grabbed some plates and silverware. Joe began to cut into the cake, but then he stopped.

"Maggie?" he said.

"Yeah, Joe?"

Joe gave a broad smile. "I'm thankful for you."

"Same here."

"I've always admired the bond between you and Grace. But now I truly understand her high regard for you. I feel it as well. You have been an absolute godsend to us. Not just through this time, but pretty much all along the way. You really *are* family."

"That means the world to me, Joe. Thanks. Now hurry up and slice that cake."

"Yes Ma'am."

They were hastened by the sound of footsteps coming from the bonus room. A few bumps, a tumble, followed by the sound of something crashing. Maggie and Joe froze as they caught one another's eye.

"Matty," they said at the same time.

"Quick, put the cake in the fridge in the garage," said Maggie.

"Wow, I don't even know if we have any real breakfast food," said Joe.

Maggie began searching in the refrigerator. "Hey, we're creative types. We'll improvise."

Within the next three hours, the house breathed life again as Maggie's parents returned and the children awoke declaring their hunger.

It would take a while before a state of normalcy could

return to the house. But the resilience was definitely there. As the house slowly came to life in the light of this new morning, it was clear that healing was certainly on the way.

# Chapter 21

aggie studied her reflection in the mirror, smoothing her hair and carefully retouching her lipstick. Richard was taking her to a benefit that evening for a children's charity that was sure to be a well attended society gathering.

He loved these kinds of events - it was a chance to see and be seen; and as usual, Maggie would serve as his compass for all the appropriate social and professional connections.

For Maggie, it was simply a night out; a chance to get dressed up, drink champagne and try and regain some sense of lightness in her life.

In the year that had passed since Grace's death, Maggie slowly began to resume the daily tasks of her world. She rejoined Deana and the band for the annual Country Music festival in downtown Nashville, as well as for various dates on the road. Deana and Charles wondered if Maggie's return was too soon, but she proved to be a master of self preservation.

Her distance and distraction were noticed by all, and while she was not unpleasant to be around, Darla, Chrissy and the rest of the band realized that the Maggie they knew had yet to fully return.

Maggie poured her heart into the music. It was a

healing balm to the wounds in her spirit. When she wasn't on stage, she was working on prose; journaling in her notebook on the road, or playing melodies on the piano at home. The work was her outlet and her salvation.

Then there were the Buchanan children. Maggie remained true to her word, stepping in when Joe found himself in a bind.

Not surprisingly, he had a never ending stream of admiring female students and neighborhood soccer moms who gladly offered their assistance. The children would politely and respectfully tolerate the presence of these women; silently counting the days until their Aunt Maggie returned from the road.

Maggie saw those children as an extension of the best of who Grace was, and she gave them everything she had.

For the children, the love was felt, received and returned in equal measure.

"Maggie? You ready? We're running late," Richard shouted from the bottom of the stairs.

Maggie gave herself a final assessment before standing back to admire her ensemble: a simple scarlet silk dress, her hair piled on her head in a confection of waves and soft tendrils that hung down around her face. She wore the earrings that were made for her - the final gift from Grace. They brought out the intricate brocade work that accented the dress.

Maggie felt as good as she looked. Her hopes for a magical evening were, for the first time in a long time, quite high.

"Maggie!" Richard yelled.

"I'm coming, I'm coming," she said, adding under her breath, "Don't worry. There will be plenty of people to suck up to. No one's going anywhere."

As Maggie reached the base of the stairs, Richard was there to greet her with his Oscar-winning smile. Resplendent in Hugo Boss, his body seemed created for no other purpose than to wear fine clothes. "Mmmm ummmph!" He said as he picked up her matching wrap to put it over her shoulders, "Talk about the best looking couple in Nashville!"

She could see their reflection in the living room window. "Yes, indeed, we are quite a pair," she cooed. A confidence she'd not experienced in some time coursed through her veins. This could be a thrilling night for the two of them. Something close to what they shared in the beginning.

And then, the real Richard resurfaced.

"That dress hugs you in all the right spots, baby," he said as he ran his hands rather crudely over her hips. "It's gonna take everything to keep me in line tonight."

While not necessarily impressed with his attempt at a compliment, it felt good to have simple admiration pointed in her direction. Kissing him on the cheek, she smiled and said, "Keep your hands where I can see 'em, my brotha."

"Sorry, can't help myself."

"Well try," she teased as she walked in the direction of the kitchen. "I'll get my keys, and we'll be off."

Just then, the phone rang. She stopped to check the caller ID out of habit. It was Joe.

"Baby, let's go," Richard said, opening the door.

Maggie hesitated before deciding to let the machine pick it up. As she reached the door, she could hear Joe's voice. There was a heaviness in it that led her to believe something was wrong.

"Hang on, Richard I just want to hear this."

Richard scoffed as Maggie returned to the kitchen to hear the message.

"Hey, you. It's Joe. Listen…um, well, you're probably busy or on the road or something, but I was hoping you could help me with…well…I'm finally gonna get rid of Grace's stuff tonight. I've been putting this off for as long as possible, and I just feel like tonight is the night to do it. Gwen won't come out of her room - she says she can't handle it - and Mom's got some big function she's going to tonight…"

"Probably the same one we're late for," Richard said. "Let's go!"

"Shhh," Maggie said, straining to hear.

"…was hoping you could give Declan and me a hand with this…and maybe even try and coax Gwennie out of her room. You seem to be one of the few people she's ever listened to." He gave out a sigh before continuing. "Now, if you're doing something important, don't you dare change your plans. Okay, call me when you can." Joe then gave an awkward chuckle. "By the way, is this an answering machine I'm talking on? Way to keep it old school, sister." Another laugh. "Thanks, Bye."

"*Way to keep it old school, sister,*" Richard mocked in an overtly sanitized manner. "Give me a break."

Maggie was torn. She and Richard both needed the night out-despite the fact that it was for vastly different reasons.

But what Joe needed to accomplish was no small task. This was an evening with which he'd been wrestling for nearly twelve months. For the first few weeks after the funeral, he couldn't bring himself to sleep in the room; much less touch any of Grace's things. He even went as far as purchasing an entirely new bed before he could sleep there again. He finally started to realize that *all* of Grace needed to be put to rest.

He just didn't have the strength to do any of it before now. Maggie knew that she needed to be there.

"Have you lost your mind?" Richard said as she backed slowly in the direction of the stairs. "Did he not just say *not to change your plans* if you're doing something important?"

"Oh, Richard, I'm sorry…but this isn't just him needing a babysitter or someone to pick up food for the kids. This is major."

"And what are we?"

"Are you seriously bringing it down to our relationship versus the Buchanans?"

"It's been nothing *but* the Buchanans, Maggie!"

"I can't believe this," she said, walking away.

Richard followed after her. "No, Maggie. This man has got friends. He's got family, he's got enough money *to hire* someone, but no, he needs his little servant…who'll step and fetch whatever, whenever he says."

"Oh you've got a lot of nerve, talking about steppin' and fetchin,'" she countered.

"What? Oh no, girl…you wait a minute…"

She held up a finger in defiance. "First of all, I am *not* your *girl.*"

"Oh, I am well aware of that," said Richard, glaring. "We all know whose *girl* you are…"

# Chapter 22

Maggie had never felt so ready to slap someone for the sheer release it could bring, but she simply responded by reducing her voice to an intense whisper.

"Secondly," she continued, "We both know that all tonight's about is you kissing up to the executives, bankers and power players. I love your ambition, Richard-but before you start throwing out some "Uncle Tom" references - you'd better take a good, long look at the bowing and scraping you do whenever we go out to these events."

Richard, at this point, was livid, but Maggie wasn't finished.

"This relationship is a *farce*, Richard Davidson, and you are, in the truest sense of the word - exhausting." The personal admissions were coming faster than she could manage to keep up. "We both know that you and I are a joke and a waste of time."

The more she spoke, the greater clarity she gained. This newfound aggression was becoming more and more like a welcome friend to her, and an undesirable foe to him. Purging herself further, she continued her attack.

"I come down stairs to yet another slew of your back handed compliments. And sadly, you think you've said enough to butter me up so I'll help you get what you need tonight at the party…and because you are so predictable, *after* the party."

She knew she couldn't slow her momentum until she was completely free. "But I'm responsible too," she went on. "I'm responsible for giving you carte blanche in my life and letting this sham go on for as long as it has."

Richard opened his mouth in protest, but Maggie put an end his response quickly. "Oh please," she said, cutting him off. "You don't love me. You don't even care about me. You can barely stand to look at me half of the time."

Maggie stopped to get her breath and regroup. This was it: the door of opportunity was open. But she needed to center herself again before she said the final thing that simply had to be said.

"Go, Richard. Go to the benefit. Have a good time. And…" her voice trailed off as she made her way to the landing. Turning to face him, she said, "You can consider tonight to be the start of our break."

Richard earnestly didn't believe she would take it to this extreme. He looked stunned. "You're seriously going to do this, aren't you?"

"Richard, I've never been more sure of anything in my life. There's nothing here for either of us. Where is this going? What are we trying for, really?"

Stuck somewhere between frustrated and furious, Richard bolted toward the door.

"I'm sorry, Richard. Really I am," she called out to him. "But you know that this is the best thing for both of us."

As he opened the door, he stopped for a parting shot. "You got that right, Maggie." His smile turned dark and malevolent as he said, "You could say that you have taken a significant, um…*weight* off of my shoulders."

Maggie winced at his obvious jab. But she wasn't going to allow the name calling to continue. "Good bye, Richard," she said calmly.

Now it was Richard's turn. He was determined to inflict as much pain as possible before his departure. The buttons he chose to press were ancient and worn, but they were always effective.

"Too bad you're not much more than a maid to those people," he said. "On the other hand, I hope you have fun - spending your time pretending to be a family; taking care of this White man's kids. God knows it's the closest you're gonna get to it, old as you are…looking like you do."

Satisfied that he'd done significant damage, Richard slowly shut the door.

# Chapter 23

Maggie paused halfway up the stairs. Placing her hand on the wall to steady herself, she drew in a deep breath and shook her head. "You are only young once, but you can be immature for life."

She didn't linger long in her thought, because there was an important appointment to keep. An appointment that required a considerable change of wardrobe.

Maggie returned the dress to the closet, removed the better part of her makeup and wound her hair into a plastic clip. Picking up her cell, she called Joe to let him know that she was on her way.

The family had already taken the time to pick out articles of Grace's that they could keep as mementos. What was left was separated into three significant groups: Joe would take his lot to Goodwill, Declan to consignment and Maggie to storage. She chose nothing to take with her. She was perfectly happy with all of the reminders of Grace she had in her world.

Gwen was curled up on her bed, iPad in hand, headphones in ears, drowning out the activity below. Hung on the back of her desk chair was the old denim jacket that her mother had worn since college. Gwen had always thought it to be the one truly cool thing that her mother owned, so that was what she chose to keep. But her sorrow at this point was too great to join the others downstairs. It was easier to retreat to her room, crank up the music and get lost in the sound. Yet another trait she'd inherited from her mother.

As she was surfing the latest updates on TMZ.com, she noticed her cell phone had an incoming text. It was from her Aunt Sissy.

Hey there sweet pea!
Hi Aunt Sissy!
How's my girl?

Gwen hesitated before answering. She simply typed - ☹.

Oh honey, you wanna talk to me about it? Sissy responded.

While Maggie was one of the few people with whom Gwen could be completely herself, she also felt perfectly safe in sharing her fears and feelings with her aunt. Her attitude lightened as she continued to chat.

Downstairs, the activity had shifted from work to dinner. Boxes had been packed in respective vehicles as Joe paid the pizza delivery man.

Juggling two large pies and a couple of two-liter bottles of soda, he yelled, "Okay everybody…come and get it! I slaved over a hot telephone to make sure this dinner got made, so come eat this food."

"Nice," Declan said as he grabbed a beer out of the refrigerator.

"You think Gwen will come down?" Maggie asked as she herded the twins to the table.

"Well, I dunno," Joe said mysteriously. "We might be able to talk her down if she knows two of her favorite things are in the kitchen."

"Oh yeah, that's right," Maggie said, catching the joke. "Pizza…and a certain tall, blonde history professor."

Declan, his face now a distinct shade of crimson, took his beer into the living room as Joe and Maggie teased him. "I'm not even part of this conversation," he said, hands in the air in surrender.

"We never intended for you to be," Maggie said as she dished out slices of pizza for the children, while subduing a spat between them at the same time.

"It's amazing," Joe continued. "You give her one stuffed pink pony for her fourth birthday, and all of a sudden she's sworn total allegiance to you. Apparently, she's got a thing for big, goofy Dutchmen."

Joe and Maggie's laughter continued as Declan leaned against the back of a sofa, crossed one long leg over the other and sipped his beer. He shook his head in embarrassment. "Spare me, please," he said.

At six feet four inches, Declan Young's blonde, athletic good looks had drawn constant offers for modeling and acting jobs from the time he was a teen. But education was his passion - coasting by on his looks was never in his game plan. He was well aware of how handsome he was, but wasn't consumed by it. Clean cut with a casual air, he had a natural ease with himself which made him that much more striking to the opposite sex.

As brilliant as he was attractive, he vigorously pursued his dual degrees in history and behavioral science. When he joined the university faculty, he and Joe became fast friends. The two men shared a love of football, politics and the music of the Eagles.

Despite Joe's obliviousness as to why his classes were so heavily populated with females, Declan knew exactly why the women flocked to his.

Just the sight of the two of them - Declan, tall and fair with his long, confident strides alongside Joe, who was slightly shorter and darker with his quick, intense steps, would cause women to stop whatever they were doing or saying until the two passed by.

Declan's take-it-or-leave-it attitude toward dating made him not quite a player, but not quite ready to be a family man either. He was a single man who enjoyed his status. He knew that he'd settle down when the right woman came along, but he was in no rush to find her.

Young Gwen was his most ardent admirer. Though she would never admit it, the crush she had on him was long standing and legendary within the family. She was silent in his presence and sad when he'd leave. Any attempt at discussing this behavior, however, would mortify her.

"All I know," said Maggie, "Is that you better watch out, Declan. Gwennie's getting more gorgeous by the second."

"Hey, don't think I've missed it," he countered, finally getting in on the silliness.

"Okay, hold up there, buddy," said Joe. "That's my kid you're talking about. I'm not above punchin' you out if you say the wrong thing!"

"Chill," said Declan. "I was just gonna say that when she grows up, she's gonna be a true beauty. Just like…"

As Declan's words stopped short, the three of them remained silent; with Maggie and Declan wondering how Joe would handle his response. Joe quickly stepped in to keep him from regretting his words. "Yes, she's gonna be a true beauty, just like her mother. Hey, don't worry," he said as he poured himself some soda. "I haven't had a dance with ol' Kentucky Thunder since that night. There's no 'deep end' to fall off of anymore. And as much as I miss her, there's so much about Grace that we still have to enjoy - like these little rascals."

Putting his soda down, Joe scooped up the kids and began kissing them to the point of annoyance.

"Dad!" they screamed. "Cut it out! Ewww!"

The increase in activity and laughter broke through Gwen's barriers, causing her to remove her earphones to investigate.

Sounds like dinner's on down there. I should probably go,

Gwen typed.

Okay, well, give your dad a big hi for me.

I sure will! Sounds like Aunt Maggie's here too.

Sissy bristled slightly at the thought.

Really? She's still coming over a lot?

Sorta. She helps out a lot when she's not on the road. I love her. She's cool.

Yes, she is cool.

Grimacing as she typed, Sissy revealed none of her angst to her niece. But Maggie's presence at the Buchanan home felt very invasive to her.

She tried to sound as cheerful as possible as she typed,

Well, give her a hello for me as well. BTW, is that hottie Declan down there too?

Gwen's heart fell into her stomach at the mere mention of Declan's name. If he was down there, she needed to fix herself up. Still not quite old enough to wear little more than eyeliner and lip gloss, there was primping yet to do. She couldn't go down there looking anything less than adorable.

The amount of time it took for Gwen to respond to the question led Sissy to believe that she'd struck a nerve. The last thing in the world Sissy wanted to do was hurt the girl's feelings.

Hey sweetie, I'm just kidding you.

That's okay. He probably is. He was helping Daddy with all that packing. I'll tell him you said hi too. Love you!!!

Thanks! I love you too!! Hang in there!!

Gwen removed her earphones as Joe knocked on the door.

"Hey sweetheart, you want some pizza?"

With much more cheerfulness than she'd expressed in some time she said, "Sure Daddy, I'll be down in a minute. I just wanna freshen up."

Her response caught Joe pleasantly off guard. "Oh…okay…great! See you in a few!"

# Chapter 24

Sissy sat contemplating the relationship she had with her sister. Certainly there was love, but the gap connecting their ages left a cool reserve between the two of them. Even though Sissy was the elder of the two, there was this sense within her that Grace was the more revered. From the moment she was born, Grace was the golden child. The preference was unintentional - but even began with her name. Grace meant *favor*, and that was exactly what she seemed to receive.

The better life, the fantastic husband, the great home, the great kids…Grace had it all. Not that her own life was anything to sneeze at - it just seemed that until the day of her death, Grace was the one with the seemingly charmed existence.

And the more she thought about it, the more Sissy continued to be annoyed by the fact that Maggie seemed to be taking up residence in her sister's home. Taking up residence in a life she believed was her own by birthright.

Now Sissy felt protective of that life. Protective of it at all possible costs.

Maggie, no matter how close she claimed she was to Grace, was not family. She was an intrusion.

"Time for me to make some changes," she said to herself as she began composing an email to Trevor Bailey-

Simmons, VP of Artist and Repertoire for Star Records, Nashville.

*Trev...*

*I've been mulling over that conversation I had with you and Lanie Hoyos last year at Virago after the CMA's. With the transitions my late sister's family is experiencing, I was thinking perhaps it was time for me to head back east. Is the offer to be on your team still open? Give me a call, any time. I'm two hours behind you, so don't worry about it being too late. You've got my cell number.*

*Look forward to talking with you soon.*

*Gwen Hammond*

As she hit "send," a smile crossed her face.

Maggie placed the final items on a shelf in the storage facility. Bringing the heavy door down to the ground, Maggie felt something shut down within her heart as well. Between her fight with Richard and the emotional toll of putting Grace's things away, she simply wanted to hide under the covers of her bed and not come out until she absolutely had to.

As she got behind the wheel of her car, she caught herself dialing Grace's cell and grimaced at the irony. "Instinct," she said, looking heavenward. "Sorry, hon."

She dialed another number while putting her car in drive. "Hi Ma, it's me. Did I wake you? No, I'm fine. I just wanted to talk."

Several days later as another birthday passed, Maggie had friendly chats with her mother, Darla and Deana; but for the most part, solitude was far more compelling. A loneliness had settled on her like she'd never felt before.

The loss of Grace came with its own initial ache, but Maggie found that it was the day to day living without her best friend that hurt most of all.

Sitting in her favorite spot in her living room at the end of the day, Maggie absentmindedly stared out the window, an open journal in her lap. Her daze was broken by the sound of the phone ringing.

"Hey Mag, it's Joe and the kids."

A smile slowly spread across Maggie's face. She figured the Buchanans would call eventually. But it was the obvious ruckus going on in the background from the kids that was truly funny.

"Shhh…stop…Matty, quit, I'm serious!" he said. "Sorry, Mags. Listen, whatever you've got planned tonight, cancel it. We're taking you out to dinner for your birthday - Matty, M&M - I *mean it...stop!* Okay, it's partly for your birthday, but mostly because my children are driving me crazy. Gwen, take that out of your brother's hand, please! Ugh! Alright Mag, We're just leaving the house now. So get ready, because we're not taking 'no' for an answer. Okay, I've got to go. It's time to kill my son. Bye!"

Maggie giggled. "Yeah, I should probably keep that from happening," she said aloud as she unfolded from the couch to change her clothes.

The activity at Shogun proved to be the one thing that could capture and hold Matty's attention. Flying shrimp, short, quick bursts of flame and plenty of theatrics on the part of the chef kept the boy mesmerized.

"My only fear is that he's gonna wanna break out the knives at home," Joe whispered to Maggie.

Maggie frowned. "Yeah, he already knows how to set things on fire," she said.

"What?!"

"Just kidding," she said laughing.

Joe peered around to look at his son, and then back to

Maggie, who had since stopped laughing. Exchanging fearful looks, they then shook their heads to reassure themselves.

"Nah, he wouldn't," Maggie said.

"Let's hope not," said Joe with a chuckle.

The whole evening lifted Maggie's spirits, particularly when they brought out her birthday cake. Maggie raised an eyebrow at the solitary candle in the center. "Only one?" she asked.

Without missing a beat, Mary Margaret said in her typically grown-up way, "Well, it's a really small cake. We figured it we put *all* the candles on, there would be too much fire."

Everyone, including Maggie, burst into laughter as Joe put his hand over his eyes in embarrassment. Maggie gathered the girl into her arms, hugging her and kissing her. "Thank you, baby," she said through laughter more jovial than she'd experienced in months. "You're always my source for reality."

✠

"So what are we doing here, Daddy?" Gwen asked as Joe pulled into a space at the Kroger parking lot.

"You'll see," he said. "Stay put and I'll be right back."

Maggie turned and gave the kids a look that said, "I have no idea what he's doing either."

Just then, a song came on the radio that Gwen really liked. Staring out the window, she began to softly sing along. The purity and beauty of the girl's tone caught Maggie by surprise. "You sound good, honey," she said.

Gwen's face took on an elated glow. "Really, Aunt Maggie?"

"Absolutely, sweetie."

"Hey! Aunt Maggie," Matty interrupted. "I can sing

too. Listen!" He began a series of vocal gymnastics that were comical and irritating at the same time.

"That's great honey. You're ready for *American Idol*. Now hush up," said Maggie. Returning her attention to Gwen, she removed her seatbelt to shift around behind her. "Seriously, is singing something you'd like to do?" she asked the child.

The question brought fresh excitement to Gwen's countenance. "Yeah!" she said brightly. "More than anything!"

"Let's talk about it later, okay? Here comes your dad."

Joe returned with two shopping bags in his arms. Passing them over to Maggie, she saw that they were full of flowers. She realized where their next stop would be. She looked at Joe and gave him a sad smile of understanding.

# Chapter 25

Keeping the kids occupied, Maggie turned up the radio and encouraged the kids to sing. They drove through the streets of historic Franklin, unaware of Joe's destination. Turning left from Hillsboro Road onto Del Rio, it suddenly became clear to them where they were going. The cemetery lay sprawling over hills to their immediate left.

As Joe made his way to Grace's burial site, the singing slowly started to fade.

"Daddy…" said Gwen, her eyes brimming with tears.

"Hey, it's been a while. We need to do this," said Joe as he parked the car. Grabbing one of the bags from Maggie's lap, he helped everyone get out of the car and ushered them to the gravesite.

A simple polished marble headstone inscribed with Grace's name was situated next to a matching marble bench. Joe gave each of the children and Maggie a separate gladiola and motioned to the stone. "If there's something you want to say, go ahead kids," he said.

Gwen stepped forward and placed her flower in front of the stone. There was a photograph of the entire family between Grace's name and the dates of her birth and death. Gwen remembered that picture. Maggie had taken it on the last Thanksgiving they'd spent together.

"Mom," said Gwen, choking back more tears. "I love you and I miss you so much. I hope you're okay where you are. I just want you to know how sorry I am for all the times I gave you grief about stuff. And I'm really taking good care of your jean jacket. Marianne Cooper was so jealous. The first time she saw me in it, she called her mom and made her buy one...but it's not nearly as cool as yours." She wiped her eyes and cleared her throat as her vulnerability began to fade. "Well, anyway, I love you. Bye."

Matty was next. As he laid down the flower he said "Hi Mama. I miss you too. Um...I thought you should know that I'm not fighting with M&M...well, not as much. And Aunt Maggie and Gramma B are making me eat all my vegetables. You'd be real proud of me..."

Everyone laughed as Matty continued on. After he finished, Mary Margaret delivered a similarly sweet and funny message as she placed her flower on top of the two flowers Matty and Gwen had left.

"I miss you, girl," Maggie said as she knelt down in front of the stone. "Nothing's the same here without you. There's so much I want to tell you. I finally dumped Richard..."

She realized her indiscretion in front of the children and covered her mouth. "Sorry, I'll save that for another visit," she said softly. "I love you."

As she rose, she grasped Joe's hand briefly to steady herself. She gathered the children around her as Joe took his turn.

"Well, guess you really are our angel now," he said. "I know you've got better things to do where you are, but should you get a chance, it would be great if you could keep an eye out over all of us. I know we'd all appreciate it...well, everyone except for Matty, I think..."

"Aw Dad!" Matty said in an uncommon moment of embarrassment as everyone else laughed.

"We'll be back soon," Joe continued. "I miss you. I love you more than life, Sweetheart."

As they headed back to the car, Gwen noticed that there was still a bag with flowers on the floor in the front. "We still have some flowers, Dad," she said. "Who gets these?"

"Why, the birthday girl, of course," Joe said as he opened the passenger door. Reaching into the bag, he pulled out a bouquet of wildflowers. "This was the only bunch of its kind in the whole place," he said as he handed them to Maggie. "I don't know; they just seemed like you."

Though Joe had no way of knowing, wildflowers were, in fact, her favorite. The varying colors, textures and hues of a simple, rustic bouquet had always captivated her. Roses were lovely, and daises were, as she heard once in one of her favorite romantic movies, the friendliest, but wildflowers looked to her how life should be: all the colors of the rainbow complimenting one another and creating something beautiful.

But flowers weren't something that came her way all that often - Richard wasn't into giving them to her, unless he'd done something wrong - and her parents were good to send her some from time to time. But other than that, no one had ever really given her any for any reason. She cradled them in her arms as they made their way back home, counting the whole evening as one of the best of her life.

# Chapter 26

Despite the change that time brings to any community, Urbana, Ohio possessed a quaint sameness to it that brought Maggie comfort each time she would visit. Labor Day was one of her favorite reasons to go home, primarily because of the annual picnic. It started as a simple event between the Wests and the Hammonds, but soon it became something of a community event, with dozens of other friends and families invited to join in the fun.

As the rural Route 68 slowly morphed into what she knew to be South Main Street, she slowed her car's speed to enjoy the brilliant colors of a Midwestern autumn.

Her ritual was always the same: she would drive past the spots that brought back the best memories of her childhood before heading to her parent's house.

This time, however, the memories were far more poignant. This was her first trip back to Ohio since Grace's death.

Her last stop before heading to her parents' home was always the corner delicatessen. For the neighborhood children, Carmazzi's wasn't so much known for its fine selections of meats, cold cuts and cheeses. As far as they were concerned, it was all about the candy. A mere dollar could provide a child with a small bag of goodies guaranteed to keep every dentist in Champaign County in business.

Stepping into the narrow space sent Maggie back in time immediately. The shelves of sweets were, as they always had been, centered in the middle of the small, busy room. Miraculously, she found most of her favorites. With each discovery, she'd say with genuine excitement, "Oh wow, they still make these!"

Taking her purchases to the register, she found a slightly older, slightly grayer Mr. Carmazzi behind the counter.

"Hey there, Mr. C," she said brightly.

"My, my, Miss Maggie West," he said in his kindly way. He knew every child by name, and never forgot a face. "You in town for the long holiday?"

"Sure am."

Carmazzi surveyed the items Maggie had chosen for herself and chuckled. "Jaw Breakers, candy buttons, Mike Sell's Bacon potato chips…some things never change."

Maggie joined him in his laughter. "Yes sir. And in this case, that is a very good thing."

"Give my best to the Judge and the Missus."

"Will do. Have a great Labor Day."

The West's house on South Walnut was much smaller when Dexter and Lenore purchased it back in the 1970's. But once prosperity asserted itself, instead of moving to a more upscale neighborhood, Dexter chose to reinvent their house with a spacious addition onto the back. The house was a clear reflection of him: refined, austere and intimidating.

She stood outside the house for a moment to admire its beauty. Noticing that her father's car was missing, but her mother's was still parked in the drive, she found her copy of their house key and let herself in.

"Ma? Daddy? Anyone home?"

No answer.

Maggie took her bags upstairs to her room. Little had changed over the years. Many of the awards, trophies and mementoes of her youth still decorated the lavender walls. Placing her bags on the bed, she realized that her mother had found some new photos and placed them in frames on top of the chest of drawers: Maggie at 16 with her first car - a '63 Ford Fairlane that all her friends called 'the batmobile", in cap and gown on graduation day with Grace, striking a pose in front of Grace's red Buick Riviera, a silly picture with Lenore and several cousins from Chicago; a more formal picture of her and Dexter taken just before Maggie left for prom.

Maggie touched the photo of her and Grace tenderly before turning away to unpack her things. She heard her parent's car pull into the driveway, and racing down stairs, she met her father at the back door attempting to balance three full sacks of groceries.

"Hey, perfect timing," she said as she took a bag out of her father's hands. "How you doin', Daddy?"

"Aww, Baby Girl," he said, placing the other two bags on the counter in order to hug his daughter. "It's so good to see you."

"Maggie! Oh honey," Lenore exclaimed as she maneuvered through the door, her own arms loaded down with bags. "I'm so glad you're home. Dexter, come on and help me now…"

Her momentary fussing at her husband gave way to her initial joy at seeing her daughter for the first time in many months. She rushed into Maggie's arms and held tightly.

"Oh, I've missed you," Maggie said.

"Me too, baby. Good to have you home."

"Look at this spread," Maggie said as she peered into the numerous bags. "This is gonna be great!"

"Yeah, girl," said Lenore. "I've got recipes for some great new salads, and of course, the old standbys."

"Your potato salad, right?" Maggie asked eagerly.

"Of course."

Dexter studied Maggie as he grabbed an orange and took a seat at the kitchen table. "What?" she asked him.

His brow furrowed, "What's happening with your hair?"

"Dexter…" said Lenore, the tone of her voice clearly expressing a warning.

Maggie checked the clock on the wall, "Wow, Daddy. That has to be a personal best for you," she said of his criticism. "Six whole minutes from the time you walked in the door. What do you mean what's happening with my hair? I straightened it, what's the big deal?"

Lenore never took her eyes off of her husband, even while addressing Maggie. "There is no big deal, honey. You look great. When you straighten it like that, you can really see how much it's grown, right, Dexter?"

"No, no, baby girl, I mean, you're mom's right - you do look great," Dexter backpedaled. "I just like it when you wear your hair with that natural curl. It's just more 'you'"

"She heard your point, honey," said Lenore.

"Well, I'm glad I can provide a little something for everyone," said Maggie with a forced cheerfulness.

The tension in the room eased somewhat as Maggie began assisting her mother in putting the groceries away.

As they sat down to a light supper, Maggie brought her parents up to speed on the events of her life of late. She regaled them with stories from the road, and how she was working on more of her own material and hoped to get her own players to showcase it soon. While he offered no questions or comments, Dexter seemed genuinely interested in what Maggie had to say. There was even a moment where she thought she saw a hint of pride.

She'd managed to leave Richard out of the conversation for the better part of the evening. Dexter seemed to take the breakup harder than Maggie, so she was determined not to mention him at all. Things stayed on a cheerful plane throughout most of the meal.

"Daddy, by the way, when I hugged you, I meant to tell you that you smell good," Maggie said. "You probably have no idea what it is you're wearing do you?"

"Girl, you know he doesn't pay any attention to that," Lenore said as she busied herself by getting more food from the stove. "I find something I think I'd like on him, hold it up to his nose, and hope he likes it too."

"Mmm, well I love it," said Maggie, leaning in to enjoy the scent again. Without thinking, she continued, "It smells like something I bought for Richard last…"

*Ugh, I knew it,* she said, mentally scolding herself. *I knew if I tried too hard not to mention him, I'd mess up. Okay, Maggie…brace yourself…here we go…*

Using her fork to shift items around on her plate, Maggie winced and refused to look up.

The tension slowly returned as Dexter said coolly, "So, the two of you are back together, then?"

"Dex," said Lenore in a cautious voice.

"Hey, I didn't bring it up," he said, as he continued to eat.

"Well, Dad, to tell you the truth, Richard and I are not back together. In fact, I've not seen him or spoken to him all summer. And I'm fine, by the way, in case you were wondering."

"What I'm wondering, is how you could let a good man like that slip through your fingers," he said.

"Dad, there was more going on than you even want to know about."

"That's all well and good young lady, but you're not too far from turning a certain age; and you really shouldn't be so choosey at this stage of your life. In relationships, you gotta take the good with the bad. Pick your battles, find that middle ground..."

"Daddy, you make it sound like we were engaged or something. I don't think we were even close to being permanent in our relationship."

"You know, Richard said he always liked your hair with that curly natural look too..."

"Daddy, are you even listening to me?" Maggie felt completely pushed to her limit.

"Excuse me, young lady?" he said.

"Dexter, calm down, and Maggie, watch your tone," said Lenore, who was determined, once again, to be the peace maker between her husband and daughter.

"Dad," Maggie said. Her outward calm was restored, but inside, she was seething. "I'm sorry I let the last possible good Black man on earth get away from me. I'm sorry my hair is such a mistake. I'm sorry I chose music over law. I'm sorry I'm fat - no, you didn't mention those things, but I know it's only a matter of time..."

"Oh Maggie," said Dexter.

Maggie rose from the table to put her dishes in the dishwasher.

"I'm sorry...I mean no disrespect. I'm just tired. I'm gonna hit the shower and go to bed early," said Maggie.

"Ma, dinner was great. Why don't you wake me up when you get up and I'll help you get the salads and stuff together for the picnic. Good night, guys."

"Good night, Maggie," said Lenore. Dexter pursed his lips and let out a low sound to signify his response.

Wearied from battle, Maggie made her way upstairs to her room. Putting a cassette tape into her antiquated boom box, she sank down into her purple bean bag chair and stared out the window. As the sounds of Atlantic Starr carried her out of her present, she could see Grace's old bedroom window. She remembered the toy walkie-talkies the two of them would use to carry on conversations at the end of the day. A tear escaped her eye as she once again wished she could talk with her best friend at that moment.

Minutes disguised themselves as hours back in the kitchen. Lenore was up, silently putting leftovers in plastic containers, forming her thoughts carefully. Before Dexter could manage his defense, she walked calmly over to him. Pointing a well-manicured nail in his face, she said firmly yet quietly, "That girl has been through more than her share of heartache this past year…"

"I know honey, but all I was trying to say was…"

"It doesn't matter, what you were *trying* to say, Dexter West," she broke in. "If that baby has one ounce of pain from you this weekend, I promise you will make your home on that couch in the den until the Lord Jesus Himself splits the clouds!"

Her work complete, she made her retreat to the television room to crochet and watch a recorded episode of her favorite soap. Dexter stayed at the table, the remainder of his dinner uneaten.

# Chapter 27

A gentle rain the night before gave way to an absolutely perfect morning. It not only seemed to wash away the Indian summer humidity, but the tension that lingered in the kitchen as well. Conversation between Maggie and her parents picked up on a pleasant note, as if nothing had happened at all. She never ceased to be amazed at how the West family had raised emotional suppression to an art form.

In truth, there was little time or space for tension, as the celebration happening in Springfield's Snyder Park that day required mental energy and physical stamina. Family upon family descended on the designated area, with children, pets and picnic paraphernalia spilling out of every car, minivan and sport utility vehicle.

As Maggie and her parents unloaded their car, Joe pulled in with his mother, Sissy and the children in tow. The car barely came to a stop before the twins and Gwen burst from its confines. "Aunt Maggie!" they cried out in unison.

"Hey," she responded, her arms open wide with genuine joy.

"Whoa," Joe scolded. "Don't knock her down, guys...calm down." His words fell on deaf ears as Maggie reveled in the love of her best friend's children.

"Nice to know they listen to their father," he said sarcastically as he placed a large cooler on a picnic table.

"Everyone knows when Maggie's here, every other adult ceases to exist," said Sissy.

"Not when it comes to their Gramma," Elise said wryly. "They always perk up when I'm around."

"That's because you threaten to cut them out of your will if they don't," Joe said.

"Whatever works."

Maggie broke free from the children's clutches to attempt to help Joe with his setup. Giving Mary Margaret a playful swat on the backside as she shooed them all toward the other playing children, she joked, "You wanna know the secret? It's because *I'm* the cool one."

"Fine," Joe said. "You wanna raise them?"

"Nope," she said with a sly smile. "That's *why* I'm the cool one. I spoil 'em, hop 'em up on sugar…then send 'em right back to you."

"Thanks so much for that, by the way."

"Don't mention it," Maggie said as she examined the various deli containers Joe had brought with him. "Wow. I can see you worked hard in the kitchen last night."

"Did you honestly think I'd subject anyone to *my* cooking?" he asked.

"Ah, yes. Good point," Maggie said.

"And that is why, on the 8th day, God created the deli department," Joe returned.

"And it was *good*," Maggie cracked.

"Can I get an amen?" Joe said, waiving his hands in the air. Maggie winced at how silly he sounded and the two of them shared a laugh.

Joe continued his unpacking for a few moments before

pausing to watch Maggie with a studied expression.

"What?" She asked, slightly uncomfortable at the scrutiny.

"No, I'm sorry - it's just…well, you look really great today."

The compliment caught her completely off guard. Somehow, she managed to mutter a soft "Um…thank you," as Joe continued his assessment in earnest.

"Yeah, I don't know if it's the shade of purple in your sweater or how you're doing your hair…" He caught himself mid-sentence. "Oh, not that you don't look great every time I see you…I mean…"

A moment of awkwardness passed into silence as he tried to regain his footing.

"You just look pretty today. I've always liked the different ways you style your hair. But today, well…it's…almost too pretty for a picnic."

The combination of sweetness and clumsiness with which Joe spoke felt like pure gold to Maggie, particularly in the light of how her father had chided her the night before. It wasn't anything elaborate; she simply softened her natural curl, fastened her hair at the crown with a barrette that allowed it to spill prettily down in back around the shoulder. But it created a youthful effect that gave her face a lovely frame.

And for the first time in her life, Maggie West actually thought she felt herself blush.

Her manner grew somewhat timid as she reached back to touch it. "Well…I, um…" she laughed a little before finally managing to say "Thanks, Joe."

"Yeah, yeah. Sure." Staring a bit longer than he'd intended, Joe quickly resumed his activity. Shaking his head, he laughed at the wave of shyness he suddenly felt.

Lenore observed everything, yet said nothing. She did, however, reach over to give her daughter a kiss on the cheek. Maggie gave her mother an inquisitive look.

"Oh, baby," Lenore said sweetly. "That was 'just because.'"

Although she was out of earshot playing with the children, Sissy envied and marveled at the breezy repartee between Maggie and Joe. There was a palpable cohesion between the two of them that had obviously developed over time.

As Joe grabbed some plates to feed the twins, he noticed that Maggie had already seen about them and was well into chiding Matty for ignoring his cucumber broccoli salad.

As he walked by, Joe gave her a good-humored nudge with his elbow. "Thanks, lady," he said with a wink.

"Habit," she said shyly. Once again, her cheeks felt flush. It was starting to confuse and frustrate her. *Okay, what is up with this blushing, girl? Snap out of it!*

Regaining her composure, she said, "This is me doing the spoiling thing, remember? You now officially have some time off, so enjoy it."

"Thanks."

"Don't mention it. Now go, before ol' Ralph Harris over there takes all that three bean salad you inexplicably love so much."

"Yes ma'am," he said.

Turning his attention to Ralph, he yelled, "Dude, back away from the three bean. I'm not gonna be as nice as I was last year and let you eat it all. I don't care if you are 75. I'll wrestle ya down, bro!"

Scattered laughter followed as Ralph put down his plate to clench his small, weathered fists into a fighting stance. Joe turned and gave Maggie a warm smile and made his way over to embrace the older gentleman.

This time, it was Maggie who found her gaze lingering.

Conversation and laughter abounded throughout the meal. Trying in vain to engage themselves in the chatter, Maggie and Joe spent more time stealing glances at one another than they did eating.

As Maggie took her opportunity to observe, she found Joe staring directly at her with his trademark intensity. The shock of their eyes meeting caused Maggie to fumble her drink, spilling it across the table. While she and several others scrambled for paper towels and napkins, Joe looked down at his plate and smiled to himself.

"I can tell who's *not* gonna be first pick for the volley ball game," someone yelled.

"Hardy har har," Maggie said, masking her inner humiliation.

By this time, it wasn't just Lenore who took note and watched with interest.

Elise walked behind her son and tugged on a lock of his hair. "Ow!" He said, as he turned around. "Ma, what are you doing?" he asked.

"That's a question I should be asking *you,* my boy," she said.

"I have no idea what you're talking about."

Elise raised an eyebrow in doubt before giving him a knowing smile and walking away.

"Get a haircut," he heard her say over her shoulder. Joe chuckled, shook his head and shoved a forkful of food in his mouth while returning his attention to whatever it was Maggie was doing.

"Okay everybody," Dexter announced. "Matt and I are going to start putting our teams together. The volleyball game begins at 4."

In keeping with the friendly rivalry between Matthew and Dexter, the volleyball game was every bit as anticipated as the cookout. During the course of the meal, the two patriarchs would steal away and begin their negotiations, assembling their teams. Once everyone had a chance to rest up from the meal, the game would begin.

One might be led to believe that for all of the strategizing that went into putting such a sporting event together, the competition would be fierce and furious.

Nothing could be further from the truth.

"Keystone cops have more coordination," Elise was once heard to say.

This year's game was no exception. More time was spent laughing at the various blunders that occurred than was spent in actual play.

Maggie took her turn to serve. "Careful, butterfingers," someone yelled from the opposing team. Maggie stuck out her tongue and blew a raspberry.

In a move that surprised everyone, the ball flew with such force and accuracy that it caused Sissy and the woman next to her to shriek and move out of its line of fire. The ball hit the ground, giving Maggie her first point of the game.

"Ladies, the trick is to actually *return* the ball," yelled Matthew to the women, who by this time were folded over, laughing at their own cowardice. "The ball is your friend," he said to them. "Come on, say it with me…"

"Looks like right now, the ball is Maggie's friend," someone else called out.

"Nice job, Mag!"

"Yeah, do it again!"

"Don't count on it," Maggie said.

"That last one was a total fluke!"

Joe positioned himself in the center of the middle row. Suddenly, out of nowhere, he felt that earlier wave of warm emotion wash over him as Maggie prepared to serve again. The childlike expression she made as she wrinkled her nose in concentration was quite endearing to him.

"Maggie," her father called out. "You can serve the ball any time before the day is over!"

A series of pictures began to flash rapidly through Joe's mind…and they all involved Maggie. All of the ways she'd come through for him; calling or stopping by with a kind word, cup of coffee or some creative invention from her kitchen. the way she loved his kids, that afternoon she spent with him when he had completely lost control over Grace's death.

Through the good, the bad, the ugly and the challenging, Maggie was always there. There was no notice too short it seemed, for her to sweep in and be the hero in his world.

It was more than simple gratitude. Something else had crept up from the basement of his spirit that had been developing for some time. It was only at that very moment that it began to take shape and demand to be recognized. His eyes widened and his jaw dropped in amazement.

"Oh, you've gotta be kidding me," he said softly.

Just then, he felt a sharp pain in the center of his forehead, causing him to lose his footing. He felt himself falling to the ground.

Maggie's serve had hit him directly between the eyes and knocked him squarely on his backside.

Following a collective gasp, there was an avalanche of

laughter and applause. Elise, who had been sitting next to Janice Hammond, reached over and patted the back of the younger woman's hand.

"Yeah, I get a feeling of pride every single time he plays, don't you?" Elise said sarcastically, as Janice wiped the tears of laughter from her own eyes.

"Good going, son!" Janice called out as a few rushed to Joe's aid.

"Way to shine, Buchanan," another person said.

"I think that's the game," said Matthew. "Congratulations, Dexter. Could somebody get a stretcher for ol' Rip Van Winkle?" he said, referring to Joe.

Sissy was first on the scene. Her desire to lend a hand seemed to border on the over-exuberant. Her help not truly helping, Joe managed to scramble to his feet on his own.

"It's okay, Sis, I've got it, thanks," he said, brushing himself off.

"You're alright?" she asked in a breathless tone.

"Aside from my ego being bruised, yeah, sure. I guess I'm alright. Thanks."

"Ooooh," she cooed, trying to examine his forehead. "Looks like it's more than your ego, Joe. I'm gonna get you some ice for that."

"That would be great."

While appreciative for Sissy's efforts, he was wondering who had replaced his strong, confident sister in law with this fawning teenager. Her sudden attention to him was strange and confusing. In fact, this whole afternoon was proving to be strange and confusing.

The twins barreled into their father, squealing with delight over his silliness. Maggie finally made her approach as the others cleared the playing field. Joe put up his hands to shield himself. "Uh uh..." he said, "You stay away from me. You, young lady, are a lethal weapon."

"Joe, I'm so sorry," she said sheepishly. She eyed the red mark that was starting to form on his forehead. "Oooh...you're gonna wanna put some ice on that."

"I've got it right here," said Sissy, approaching with a full towel.

"Thanks, Sis," Joe said, his focus still clearly on Maggie.

Placing the towel in his hands, Sissy slowly began to feel as though she were a bit out of place in the conversation. Sensing her job was finished, she simply said, "Anytime, Joe," and backed away.

"Good thing your hair covers it," Maggie said. "You're gonna have a hard time explaining that to everyone at school."

"I'll just tell them I left the other guy looking a whole lot worse."

"Hey," she said, pretending to be offended.

"Come on," he said. "We both know that's a great big lie."

Playfully, he put his arm around her neck, forcing her head into his chest. The unexpected force caused her to let out a muffled cry.

"Jose, we're a little too old for noogies here...ahhhrrgh!" she managed to call out.

"Sorry," he said, letting her go. "I don't want to be responsible for messing up that pretty 'do.'"

Maggie brushed her bangs out of her eyes and laughed, "And we both know *that* happened a long time ago."

Standing practically toe to toe, they suddenly found themselves at a loss for words. Joe ran his hands through his hair the way he always did when he didn't know what to do with them. The front of his hair slicked back, made damp from the sweat he'd worked up, as well as the towel that Sissy had given him. Maggie reached out to inspect the red mark on his forehead once again.

"Looks like it's getting better," she said, her eyes moving down to meet his gaze.

"Yeah, guess so."

The feeling of awkwardness returned; but for Joe, it had definition. He was becoming infatuated with this woman. He had known her for years and had always found her to be one of the most delightful individuals he'd ever met. But today was the first day he truly *saw* her. Getting to know her on a deeper level suddenly became a priority.

As he reached over to pull some grass off of the collar of her sweater, Maggie felt no desire to look or back away from him. She was beginning to feel comfortable, not just in the cross-hairs of his gaze, but in her own skin as well. She thought that she could stare at this man for hours and constantly discover something new.

The air around the two of them had become a heady, dizzying field of electricity that swirled around them like a cocoon. Neither of them wanted to escape.

# Chapter 28

D addy. Daddy," Matty yelled again; his volume was so loud that it caused the two of them to jump a step backward. "Can we have some of Grandma Janice's apple pie now?"

Joe recovered quickly and shouted back, "Why are you yelling? I'm right here."

"Sorry," Matty said, reducing his voice to that loud whisper only children could do well. "Can I have some pie now? I promise I ate some green stuff. Tell him, Aunt Maggie."

Having stepped out of whatever force field they'd found themselves, Maggie was able to regroup. "Um, yeah," she said with a slight chuckle. "He did. I forced it down his throat myself."

"Well, kudos to you, for the eating," said Joe to Matty. Turning to Maggie he said, "…and kudos to you for the forcing. How 'bout it, Miss West - could I interest you in some of Janice Hammond's prize winning apple pie?"

"We picked the apples out of Grandma Janice's tree ourselves," said Matty as he took Maggie's hand to guide her to the table.

"Yeah, then we sold 'em to her for 50 cents a pound," said M&M.

"You what?" Joe exclaimed.

"Yeah," said Matthew, "They made a small fortune off their grandparents, for sure."

"Well, that explains the surplus of pies this year," Joe said, scratching his head. "You actually gave these two little con artists money…and then made them pie?"

The Judge and his wife looked at one another, shrugged, and laughed out loud. "I guess so," Janice said.

"You say 'con artist,' I say *entrepreneur,*" said Matthew.

"Suckers," Joe said, diving into his own slice. As usual, it was all-American perfection. "Mmm," he said, his mouth still full. "Good pie, though."

"You just wait, young man," Janice cautioned. "You'll do the same for your grandkids some day."

Joe allowed his mind to drift at the thought of his children all grown up, having children of their own. He could see growing old in the light of the myriad possibilities his offspring could contribute to the world over the course of time.

Suddenly, his mental cinema became obscured. Liquid and light, a ghost glided by, flowing in a breeze much cooler than the autumn winds he'd been experiencing all day. He could feel a feminine presence move past him…and thought could actually smell the scent of Paloma Picasso over the russet leaves and Midwestern earth.

"Joe? You okay, son?" Matthew asked.

He opened his eyes with a slight shudder. "Oh, yeah…yeah, I'm fine. Sorry."

"Hey, buddy. It's okay to think about her and still have a good time."

Joe's eyes narrowed in slight discomfort as Matthew continued. "I miss my Gracie some days so bad I don't know what to do. That's usually when Mother sends me out to mow the lawn or run an errand. Anything to keep me distracted, ya know?" he said with a smile.

Joe laughed softly. It felt good to be understood and excused for attempting to move on with life. But now, the timing of this new fascination felt completely off. *It was nice*; he rationalized to himself, *but now is just not the right time...I think...*

Maggie felt the shift from across the picnic table. She could hazard a guess at where his mind went, and felt that it was probably for the best. To her, Joe was Grace's husband, period. To hold tightly to that truth would alleviate any confusion for her in the future.

At long last, the day was over. The Wests and the Hammonds unloaded their cars of Tupperware, grills and sleeping children and began saying their goodnights.

"Ow! Matty, wake up! You know I can't carry you," Janice exclaimed from somewhere inside the car.

"Did he kick you?" Joe and Maggie asked simultaneously. They looked at one another in response and shared an awkward laugh.

Janice walked toward them, rubbing her arm. "No, just a punch this time. But I wouldn't be surprised if he left a bruise. That kid is lethal when he sleeps."

"Yeah, you need a suit of armor if you want to get him up from a sound sleep. I'll handle this," Joe said. In a whiny voice he added, "Pray for me."

As the battle to get Matty out of the car continued, Sissy made her way across the yard to talk to Maggie.

"Come here and give me a hug girl," Maggie said casually to Sissy. "It was so good to see you!"

Several inches taller than Maggie, Gwyneth Hammond bent slightly and enveloped the smaller woman. "Oh my gosh, you too!"

"Did you have fun? It's been too long since you've been

able to attend one of these."

"I sure did. I'm glad our folks decided to start it up again. It's a great way to move on from…well, you know."

"Yeah," Maggie said. Grace was never far from her thoughts, but for the past several hours it felt as though her presence was aggressively asserting itself.

"And you know, it was so great to spend time with Joe and the kids," Sissy said rather wistfully as she looked in the direction of her parents' house. Suddenly, her face brightened, and her tone became chipper. "Oh, and by the way," she said. "I don't know if you've heard…but I'm moving to Nashville."

"Really?" Maggie said, genuinely surprised at the news. "No, I guess I hadn't heard. New job?"

"More like a lateral move. There was an opening in the A & R Department at the Nashville headquarters, and I thought - what better opportunity to be closer to my family?"

"Well, it makes sense," Maggie replied. Still a bit surprised by the news, a feeling of inexplicable trepidation sprang within her.

"Yeah, Joe's really thrilled," Sissy continued. "It was such a relief to him knowing that I was coming. You know, because of the kids and him needing help and all. Not that you're not doing a great job in that department - it's just that Joe was saying the other day how much he's come to depend on you, and it would be good to have me in town so you could, um, you know…not have to shoulder that burden so much."

It was at that moment that Maggie was able to precisely pinpoint what she'd been sensing: Sissy was marking what she perceived to be her territory. "The kids are anything but a burden," she said sweetly.

"Oh I know!" Sissy exclaimed. "But I'm sure you'll be looking forward to having your life back, once more of Joe's family gets to town."

There it was again. That line of division. The 'family' card. Why Sissy continued to draw it in this passive/aggressive manner was mysterious and maddening. What was Sissy not telling her?

Still, Maggie managed to keep her cool. "It will be good to have you in town. I'm sure we'll be seeing a great deal of one another."

"Oh, you can count on it." Sissy's response carried with it equal parts promise and threat. And she knew her words had hit the mark. She reached out to hug Maggie once again. "Well, I'd better help Joe get those kids to bed…get a jump start on my Nashville duties, right?"

"Right. Well, have a safe trip and a safe move. Sissy," Maggie said. "Let me know if you need anything; a place to crash, leads on apartments…"

"I'm sure I'll be fine. I'll be staying at Joe's till I find a place, so there's no need to trouble yourself with any of that. But I will be glad to do the lunch thing with you. I'll be in touch," she said as she waved and made a sprint across the yard to the house.

Maggie stood motionless for the longest time, trying to make sense of what had just happened. Apparently a gauntlet had been thrown. Baffled by the sophomoric nature it all, she chuckled to herself and went back to helping her parents unload their car.

# Chapter 29

The halls of Timmons Entertainment in the heart of Music Row always vibrated with excitement - a testament to the momentum of Deana's career.

As Maggie walked through the door, she immediately found herself dodging a couple of interns who were in the middle of transitioning from a brisk trot to an all out run.

"Whoa," Maggie said as she plastered herself against a wall for protection. "Walk much?" she joked.

A petite, fashionably styled blonde spun around and recognized Maggie, while the young man with her stayed his course and rounded the corner of the hallway. "Oh my gawd," the girl said in a Louisiana-tinged drawl. Not slowing for a moment, she called out as she ran backwards down the hallway. "I'm so sorry, Miss West!"

"No Problem, Theresa," Maggie said. "It's good to see you, even if you're only a blur going by."

"Good to see you too….late to a strategy meeting. Talk to ya later!"

"*Run Forrest*!" Maggie teased as the girl broke into a sprint. Smoothing out the jacket of her suit, she turned her attention to a friendly-looking young man behind a large ornate desk. "Hey, Louis," she said. "Seems like everything's kicked into high gear already."

"Isn't that always the way around here?" Louis replied.

"So, how are your wife and your new baby?"

Louis simultaneously tapped in numbers on a phone while handing Maggie a framed photograph. "Getting sweeter all the time," he said brightly. Maggie examined the photo with delight as Louis alerted the party on the other end of the phone to Maggie's arrival.

"Louis, she's gorgeous," she said.

Louis beamed with pride. "Thank you very much. And Deana and Charles are in the conference room. They're waiting for you."

She bade farewell to Louis and made her way down the brightly lit corridor that led to a set of large, ornate double doors.

Styled to balance hard business with comfort, Timmons Entertainment's official meeting area was segmented into two distinct parts. At one end was a large mahogany table of oval shape, with twelve large office chairs around its perimeter. A wall of cabinets which matched the wood of the table concealed a state-of-the-art audio/visual system. Situated on the opposite side was a wet bar; beyond that a more comfortable, informal living room setting with a sofa, oversized chairs with matching ottomans, all of which centered around an always-working fireplace.

Deana and Charles occupied the sofa, sipping coffee and chatting amiably. Upon seeing Maggie, they rose to their feet, with Charles managing to get around the sofa to greet her first.

"There she is!" he exclaimed as he pulled her into a hug from a handshake. "How ya doin' Miss Maggie?"

"Hey sugar!" Deana said as she reached her, waiting her turn to give Maggie her own hug. "Thanks for coming out. It's so good to see you."

"Can I get you some coffee? Bottled water? Perrier?" Charles asked.

Maggie chose the sparkling water, and took her place in one of the oversized chairs.

"So, what is it that summons me to the inner sanctum?" Maggie asked.

Never one to stand on ceremony, Charles chose to get right down to business.

"Now Maggie, I don't wanna keep you in suspense…"

"We love you so much and are so glad that you're part of what we do here…" Deana was stopped short by her husband's stare.

"Darlin'…I got this," Charles said to her. While visibly offended by her husband's dismissal, Deana gestured toward Maggie as if to say, *Fine, go ahead.* Charles patted his wife's knee and returned his attention to Maggie.

"Anyway, hon, as you know, we're getting ready to lose Bobby. He's going to play keyboards for that new teenager they're groomin' to be the next Taylor or LeAnn or whatever."

Maggie's eyes widened in shock. It seemed as though surprises and revelations were coming at lightening speed these days. "I had heard through the grapevine that it was a possibility, but had no clue that anything was definite."

"Well, "Deana piped in. "It's definite. And his departure couldn't come at a more inconvenient time."

"As you know, Deana wants to get into the studio just before Christmas, and between her stops on *Letterman, Ellen, The View* and her Opryland gig, she's swamped," Charles said as he rose from his place on the sofa. Pouring another mug of coffee, he said without turning around, "Dee Dee and me…well, we thought you would be the best person to take Bobby's place."

Maggie nearly choked on her Perrier. "You…ahem…want me to become your Music Director?"

"And the band leader on the road," Deana added. "It only makes sense, Maggie. You're the one that knows these songs inside out."

"Maggie," Charles said. "*Time To Let Him Go* was one of the biggest albums and singles of last year…not to mention part of one of the best tours we've ever had. You were a huge part of that success. The band loves you and respects you…"

"And of course we would compensate you for the new duties…" Deana's interruptions truly aggravated Charles, who flashed her yet another impatient look. But Deana wouldn't be silenced this time. "Charles, that's enough," she said. "This is not just your show. I'm the one who is out there doing the work, my name is on the checks; there is no crime in my taking part in this conversation. I'm not just here to take up space, you know."

"Hey guys, c'mon," Maggie joked, hoping to lighten the mood. "You two are starting to sound just like my parents."

The comment achieved the desired result: The Timmonses both laughed out loud. "Well, as you can see, we're both really passionate about what we believe is best for this organization," Charles said with a diplomatic tone.

"I'm really honored," said Maggie. "Can I get some time to think about this?"

This time, it was Deana and Charles's turn to be surprised. "Uh, yeah. Sure," said a bewildered Deana.

"With all due respect, Maggie, I'm not quite sure what you'd need the extra time for," said Charles. "You do know that there are folks in this town would give their right arm for a chance at what we're offering you, don't you?

"Oh yes, I do! Please. It's not that I don't appreciate it," Maggie pleaded. "It's just that I've been working on stuff lately. Really, really good stuff…"

"You mean songs of your own?" asked Charles.

"Yes," Maggie replied.

Charles placed his coffee mug on an end table and adjusted the rim of his Nashville Sounds cap. "I think that's great, Maggie," he said slowly. "It's good that you've got a creative outlet to work on the side when you're not on the road with us."

"This is more than an outlet, Charles," said Maggie. "You know I love it here, but I was kinda hoping to strike out on my own eventually."

From the moment he brought Maggie into the band, Charles knew that this conversation was inevitable. But with everything his wife stood to achieve at this stage of her career, he needed to do everything he could to hold this team together. Bobby, he could afford to lose. Maggie was another story.

"Define 'eventually,'" he said soberly.

Maggie could feel the tension rise in the room. "Um…I was thinking…over the course of the next year," she said tentatively.

"How old are you, Maggie?"

The bluntness with which he asked the question drew a look of shock from Deana, but she stayed silent, waiting to see what her husband was going to do next.

Although she felt internally what registered on Deana's face, Maggie never changed her expression.

"You know how old I am, Charles. What does that have to do with anything?"

"I'm not saying you're old. In fact, I'm being completely honest when I say that you look almost exactly the same as you did the first day I saw you. You're a beautiful girl. But you know that recording contracts don't come easily to anyone over the age of 22. And last I checked, you're way past 22."

Maggie let out a heavy sigh. The sound of the imaginary sand running out of the imaginary hourglass was deafening.

Charles strode across the room on long legs and sat on the ottoman in front of Maggie's chair. Taking her by the hand he said, "I'm not trying to discourage you from chasing a dream. But you've got it good here. Why would you wanna mess that up to take a leap off of a cliff you're not sure you'd survive? This is an ugly business in a hard town. Sure you're talented. But in music industry years, you're not a hot property. That's just the reality of it."

"Maggie," Deana said, hoping to soften the blow Charles had just administered, "We're offering you the opportunity of a lifetime. But I understand the depth of your dream. Heck, it's following those same dreams that got me to where I am today. All we're asking you to do is to think about our offer. You'll have plenty of time to do your side projects, just like always. Who knows? Maybe Charles and I could put in a good word later on down the road."

Completely deflated, all Maggie wanted to do was leave the room and go home. Charles said, "Aw, Maggie - this was supposed to be an upbeat meeting. We didn't mean to hurt your feelings."

"No, don't worry about it. Sometimes the truth hurts," Maggie said, smiling brightly, fighting back tears. Determined that they not see her cry, she bought herself some time by standing up and finishing what was left of her mineral water, and finding the wastebasket to throw it away. Donning large sunglasses that masked the disappointment in her eyes, she plastered on a confident smile and slipped the strap of her purse over her shoulder. "I'm okay. I just have some thinking and praying to do."

"And we'll be praying right along with ya," Charles said as he followed her to the door. "Seriously, Maggie - thanks for taking the time to come out. I hope you know that we really hoped we'd be makin' your day with this news."

Maggie stood in the open doorway, her hand on the knob. "I know. And hear me when I say that I truly appreciate it and am so honored. It's all gonna work out the way it's meant to in the end. So, thank you. You're right. There are a million people who'd sell their souls for this chance. I'll see you guys at the buses next week."

Deana stood in front of the fireplace, turning around just long enough to say good bye to Maggie as she left. Turning back toward the fire, she said softly, "I have no idea how to respond to what just happened here."

Charles walked behind his wife and put his hands on her shoulders, rubbing up and down her arms. "Baby…"

"Ugh. Whenever you start a sentence with 'Baby', I just know a snow job is not too far behind. So spare me the 'Baby,' okay?

Charles spun Deana around gently and kept his hands on her petite shoulders. "Listen, *Baby*…I love you, and I believe in what we're doing here. And I will do whatever it takes to keep this boat going on its course."

"But we just broke that poor girl's heart…made her doubt the very talent you're trying to hold on to."

"Dee, listen to me," he said softly. "You're fantastic. A true star. But Maggie gives you that edge that's just not out there in the marketplace today. You and I both know that we cannot afford to lose that right now. And if we have to hurt her feelings a little to make our case, so be it. It's business."

"So much for *Family First*," she said remorsefully as she freed herself from his grip and walked away.

"It *is* family first, Dee," Charles said. "*You* are my family. And you come first."

# Chapter 30

Maggie sat silently in her car for the longest time, her head resting on the steering wheel. Her thoughts were invaded by the sound of her cell phone's ringtone. She drew in a breath and answered without looking at her caller ID.

"Maggie West."

"My goodness, so professional," said the voice on the other end.

"Joe?"

"Yeah, it's me. How are ya? You sound kinda down."

Despite the ambiguous dance they'd entertained at the Labor Day picnic, the sound of Joe's voice at that moment felt good to Maggie's shattered spirit.

"Oh, it's nothing. Just another challenging day here in Music City."

"Feel like escaping the rat race to visit us common folk?"

"Sure. What's on your plate tonight?"

"An emergency meeting of the disciplinary committee. Can you believe it? We're barely through mid terms."

"Sounds intense. You need me to bring dinner for the kids?"

Joe winced in embarrassment at Maggie's insight. "Do you mind? I'll pay you back-promise."

"It's my pleasure. Don't sweat it."

Watching the children was the diversion Maggie needed to wash away the day's disappointment. Stopping by the grocery store, she decided to indulge the Hammond kids by making them each their favorite dish: broiled chicken breast and baked potato for Gwen, fish sticks for Mary Margaret and chicken nuggets for Matty. And against her better judgment, she bought the makings for banana splits as well.

After the twins began their sugar freefall, they were entertained at bedtime by one of Maggie's off-the-cuff fairy tales. Then she made popcorn and enjoyed *The Last of the Mohicans* on DVD with Gwen, who tried to talk Maggie into letting her stay up until her father returned from his meeting. But Maggie was undeterred, sending her to bed promptly at 9:30.

The house now silent, Maggie took the opportunity to spend some time on the family piano. Turning the lights off in the various rooms downstairs, there was nothing left but the glow of the tiffany lamp that rested over the Steinway baby grand.

The piano was the first truly extravagant purchase that Maggie had made for the Hammonds: a gift to them from the first royalty check she'd received after writing a few hits for Deana. Every year, she arranged to have the instrument tuned so that the children could practice their own craft.

Tenderly running her hand along the maple finish in the way one might along a lover's cheek, she paused to remember the moment the family was surprised with her purchase. It was a truly elegant piece of work that she loved even more than the upright she kept in her own home.

She never noticed Joe's car coming up the drive, and never heard him enter his home. As soon as he opened the door, he smiled at the sound of her playing. He followed the notes to the living room and stood quietly behind her, leaning against the wall. As much as he wanted to pull away and leave her to her passion, he found himself too drawn by the moment, too drawn by his attraction to her. The enormity of his past and his present colliding in the doorway of the living room brought him to a paralyzing point that he found impossible to leave.

Maggie's sonata eventually came to an end. For the longest of moments, she sat at the piano, the strains of her music still hanging in the air. When her head finally lifted, she saw the image of Joe standing behind her reflected in the windows of the living room.

Startled, she instinctively clapped a hand over her mouth, muffling a scream that caused them both to jump.

"Joe! How long have you been back there?" she asked between breaths.

Joe couldn't control his laughter. "Holy cow, somebody needs to switch to decaf," he said.

Maggie got up from the bench and gave him a slap on the arm. "Jerk," she said, now laughing herself.

"Ow! Must you always be so brutal?"

"Only when creepy, stalkerish people are around," she said. Pulling herself together, she asked, "How was the meeting?"

Joe allowed Maggie to pass by her and the two of them headed back to the kitchen. "Yes, the tribunal has decided that there will be a beheading in the public square tomorrow morning, promptly at 9 am."

Maggie rolled her eyes. She was one of the few who truly loved Joe's flair for the dramatic. "Okay, I'm kidding," Joe said as he pulled a soda from the refrigerator. Offering it to Maggie as he retrieved his own he said, "It was actually kind of pitiful. We had to question a Pre-med student who, as it turns out, was just this side of failing English Lit. Kid got caught getting texts from another student.

"Wow," she said. "High tech cheating. Do you know who the other student was?"

"Uh huh. His older brother. Apparently he had fared better in the class and had been feeding the kid brother info all semester."

"You have got to be kidding me. So what's gonna happen?"

"Normally, it would be an automatic failure."

"Normally?"

"Yeah, but as it turns out these particular students are the sons of a major player on the University board."

Maggie understood the political tone of Joe's response. "I take it you were advised to merely give a slap on the wrist," she asked.

"More like a mild tap."

Joe sat down on one of the chairs at the kitchen table. Taking a sip of his soda, he placed the can on the table and stretched his arms and legs. "Ugh. That's about four hours of my life I'll never get back."

"I'm sorry," Maggie said earnestly.

Joe opened his eyes and leaned over the kitchen table. "You in a hurry to go home?"

"Nope."

"Do me a favor?"

"I'll try."

"Play something else for me? It's a real treat to hear that piano used for something other than M&M butchering *Fur Elise* or Gwennie trying to write love songs that she swears aren't about Declan."

"Happy to oblige, my friend."

Maggie returned to the piano and started in on another piece she been working on for her collection. For a moment, Joe placed his head in his hands and absorbed the beauty of the sound. Then he had an impulsive thought. Moving into the den, he began to start a fire in the fireplace. By the time she'd reached the end of the song, Joe had created a cozy scene in the next room, complete with a newly opened bottle of wine. Maggie turned around and was impressed by the scene.

"How nice," she said. "But it's October in Tennessee, Buchanan. Still a little too warm for a fire, don't you think?"

"Don't spoil the mood, West. Care to join me?"

She did. The two of them chatted well into the night. They discussed the kids; the heartbreak of Maggie's encounter with the Timmonses earlier that day, and Joe's disappointment over the behavior of his student and the subsequent lack of discipline that the boy received.

When Maggie spoke, Joe listened. When Joe opened his heart, Maggie gave him her full attention. Neither tried to "fix" the other - and that was the beauty of it. They both reveled in the freedom to simply be themselves, warts and all.

Maggie looked at her watch and rose to collect her belongings. "Oh gosh, I should get going."

"2:00? Wow. I didn't realize we'd been talking that long."

"Neither did I," she said. Thanks for this. I had a great time. But it's got me concerned..."

Joe looked confused and a bit worried. "Concerned about what?"

"This isn't the way you pay all of your babysitters, is it?"

"Of course it is. Why waste ten bucks an hour when

you can create this atmosphere for half the price?"

Maggie feigned disgust. "Alright, first of all, please don't tell me that you actually pay your students ten lousy bucks an hour to watch those three hooligans upstairs."

"Why? Is that too much?"

"That is so sad, Joe Buchanan." Maggie picked up the bottle of what she knew was a very expensive Barolo from the cellar, but continued to joke, "I knew you were cheap. Just what was that swill you served me tonight, huh? One of those wines mixed with fruit juice or something?"

"Shut up."

The two of them started laughing. "Okay," Joe said. "Never you mind, missy. I'll just consider that little crack a payback for scaring you when I got home," Joe said.

Once again, they found themselves in the place where time stood still. Maggie leaned against the doorway of the den, hands behind her back, staring shyly at the floor. Joe stood doing the exact same thing on the opposite side of the doorway - but his eyes were fixed on her. He didn't want her to leave, nor did she have any desire to go.

"Have I ever told you how very much I'm glad you're in my life…well, our lives?" Joe said.

"That goes double for me," she said, finally looking up at him.

"Do you always have to one-up me?" Joe said, cracking a joke to mask his nervousness.

"No, of course not. But then again, it's not really a one-up when you know you're superior." With a wink and a turn, she headed toward the front door. "See you later," she said saucily.

Joe watched Maggie as she made her way to her car - partly to ensure her safety, partly because watching her had become one of his favorite things to do.

"Maggie West," he said softly as she drove into the

night. "When did you become such an adorable little flirt?"

# Chapter 31

I would like to propose a toast." Dexter stood from his seat at one end of the Buchanan's massive dining room table, his voice deepening with judicial authority. "To the hands that prepared this magnificent meal. Elise, I'm looking forward to my very first taste of your fried turkey…"

"Dex, please, we've already prayed. Speed it up, before we have to reheat everything in the microwave," said Lenore.

"Now hang on, Lenore, you'll appreciate this," he said, puffing out his chest to call attention to the Ohio State University logo emblazoned across his hand-knit sweater.

Wearing his favorite University of Michigan jogging suit, Matthew let out an exaggerated sigh and said, "Oh please!"

The rest of the family laughed, more out of obligation than actual amusement, as each Thanksgiving brought the same Ohio State/University of Michigan trash talk. Dexter continued as he raised his glass even higher.

"I would like to give thanks for the greatest coach in all of college football…"

"The late, great Bo Schembechler!" Matthew exclaimed.

Maggie and Joe's eyes met from their respective ends

of the dining room table with expressions that said, "Here we go again."

"Oh, now, hush, ya big sore loser," Dexter said. "Here's to Urban Myer. Long may he continue to lead our beloved Bucks to victory over 'that team up north.'"

"Amen," said Lenore. "Now, shut up, make yourself useful, and start carving that bird!"

As was the custom, dinner was a glorious event, made more special by the fact that Joe had opened his home to the Wests as well as his in-laws. His motive was completely ulterior - he simply wanted to be near Maggie. But it was great having the families all together again.

Almost all together.

After what they all declared was the best thanksgiving dinner yet, Maggie took time to clear some of the empty platters from the table. Joe followed her into the kitchen asking over his shoulder, "Who wants coffee?"

Maggie was rinsing a off a plate when Joe intentionally bumped her as he passed. "Hey," she said, trying to look stern. "Watch it! I'm workin' here."

"Sorry," he said, after knocking into her a second time to reach into a cabinet. "I forgot the filters."

"Yeah right. I don't think I heard anyone say that they actually wanted coffee."

"I know."

"So, what are you doing?"

"I dunno," he said with the tone of a schoolboy on the verge of punishment. "You never know. There might come a time in the evening when someone might want something...*hot.*"

Maggie raised an eyebrow at Joe's directness. It had been quite some time since any man had paid her genuine attention; even longer since she'd had intimacy on any level. Standing as close as she was to Joe at that moment, she'd never prayed harder for Christmas and the presence of mistletoe.

"Oh, well, that makes sense," she said softly. "I could definitely see where someone might need something... hot."

Tilting his head to the side as if to get a better look at her, Joe reached up to push an errant strand of hair away from Maggie's face. The effect of his contact and the fact that she had absolutely no idea what was going to happen next was nothing short of thrilling.

Her heart raced as she saw his eyes escape her gaze to concentrate on the shape of her mouth. His mind reeled as he took a tiny step closer to her, their bodies inches from touching.

*...this is really gonna happen, here? Now?*

Joe chuckled at the tiny breath that escaped Maggie as the questions burned inside her head.

The sound of the doorbell escaped their notice, but Maggie's head did an abrupt snap in the direction of the front door when she heard Dexter's hearty greeting...

...to Richard.

She went to the kitchen door and peered around, hoping she couldn't be seen.

"What in God's name is he doing here," she groaned as she rested her forehead against the doorway.

Dexter led Richard through the front door and reintroduced him all around. Lenore, unaware of the invitation, successfully veiled her deep concern by offering to fix Richard a plate. "Thank you, Mrs. West, everything smells terrific," he said.

Lenore caught Dexter's eye as she left for the kitchen. After four decades of marriage, he knew the look he was getting. *This plan had better work*, he thought to himself.

Joe hung behind as Maggie slowly emerged from her place of safety. "Richard," she said.

In two strides, Richard reached Maggie and scooped her in a warm embrace. "Maggie! This is wonderful. How are you?"

"Surprised," she said, throwing her own look toward Dexter as she returned his hug. "Happy Thanksgiving."

Richard pulled her back and took a long look at his ex girlfriend. "You too. My, my…you look good!"

"Forgive me if this sounds abrupt, but…what are you doing here?"

Richard laughed aloud. "I'm sure this must seem strange, but I got a call from your dad a couple of weeks ago, and he told me that if I didn't have any plans for the holiday, that I was welcome to come by here."

"He did, did he?" Maggie asked.

"Well…I figured that a fine, dashing, man about town wouldn't have needed to stop by. It was merely a suggestion," said Dexter, stepping forward and putting his arm around Richard.

How could I resist?" Richard said. "There were so many warm family moments that I've experienced with you all…and it was a chance to see you, again, Maggie." His smile was sweet and seemingly earnest. But Maggie was convinced something was up. In her soul, she knew two things: That when it came to her relationship with Richard, her father was like a dog with a bone, and that nothing positive could possibly come from it.

Sissy had spent much of the evening sulking over the bonding between Joe and Maggie, but Richard's arrival put an immediate bounce in her spirit. Leaning on the wall next to Joe, she said in his ear, "So, this is the infamous

Richard," she whispered with delight. "Very Nice. Who on earth would let *him* go?"

As buoyant as Sissy had become, Joe felt his own hopes take a slight dive. "Interested?" he asked with a less than upbeat attitude.

"Oh, not for me, but this could be a nice little reunion for him and Maggie."

"You don't know him," Joe said cautiously.

"Well, that's a West family situation," Sissy said. "Not our business."

"My house, my friend, my business," Joe said, walking into the dining room to greet Richard. *Best to keep one's friends close and one's rivals closer*, was his thought.

Sissy tried to call after him, but he went quickly out of earshot.

As Richard dove into his dinner, Dexter and Lenore sat on either side of him, catching up on the events of his life since parting ways with Maggie. And while Maggie took a few moments to speak to him in passing, she spent most of the evening occupying her time with Joe and the children in every other available room.

Forty-five minutes into Richard's visit, Dexter had reached the end of his patience with his daughter. He cornered Maggie in an upstairs hallway as she emerged from the bathroom. "Young lady," he said sternly. "What do you think you're doing?"

"You have *got* to be kidding me. I might ask the same question of you."

"You don't have the right to ask me anything," Dexter retorted, "I am your father. And if you're not gonna have the sense to see a gift staring you right in the face, then it's up to me to help you!"

"Daddy, you have gone too far!" Maggie said, her voice

lowered to a whisper with the intensity of a shout. "I cannot believe you! I've told you for months that Richard and I are not meant to be together. What is it going to take to get you to understand that?"

"Um, guys?" Lenore said, quickly ascending the stairs to meet them on the landing. "I know you think you're whispering, but we can hear that something tense is happening up here."

"Mom, please help me out here," Maggie pleaded. Dexter merely folded his arms and dared his wife to defy him. But Lenore was determined to diffuse the situation as quickly as possible.

"Maggie, go downstairs and at least talk to the man. No one is saying you have to marry him."

Maggie's mouth dropped in shock as Dexter said, "Thank you! That's all you've got to do: Go downstairs."

"You really don't want to risk your life by speaking any further," Lenore said, making her emphasis clear by once again pointing her index finger in his face. "Maggie, go. Now."

Maggie returned to join the rest of the eavesdropping group, who quickly rushed back to their previous places upon hearing her descend the steps.

Dexter, in the mean time, tried to defend his actions to his wife. "Honey…"

"Stop. Do not speak," she said. "I know what you were trying to do, but you have got to let that child live her life. We've been over this a million times! When are you going to get it through that head of yours that she doesn't want this man?"

"But the last time I spoke with him, he mentioned how much he missed her and how good it would be to see her again. I honestly didn't think he'd come."

Lenore sighed and took her husband's hand. "I know honey. Your heart was in the right place. But she's not 17 anymore. Please…let this obsession go, okay?"

Dexter knew he was on the ropes on the issue and nodded his head in agreement. "And one more thing," Lenore said.

"What's that?" said Dexter.

"Next time you pull a stunt of that magnitude, *warn a sistah*. You and I are a team, remember?"

"I really wanted to tell you, but I was certain that if I did, you'd tell me how foolish I was being."

Lenore put her hands on her hips and shook her head. "That'll teach you," she said laughing. "There is a reason for that verse in the Bible that says, *he who finds a wife finds a good thing*. You'd do well to remember that."

Joe watched with a degree of disappointment as Maggie fixed herself a soda and sat with Richard as he finished his meal. Maggie still felt that undefined knot in her gut, but she chose, for the sake of peace, to try and ignore it.

"So, Miss Maggie," Richard said, laying his fork down. "If your ears were burning last week, there was a good reason for it. I was talking about you."

"Oh Lord," Maggie said lightly.

"No, no, it was a good thing," Richard said. "Just a mutual friend of ours - Joe Jackson."

"Really? I remember introducing you at the Grammy after party, but I didn't know you were all that chummy with the president of Athens Entertainment."

"Well, my dear," he said raising his wine glass, "That's because of you. He is now a solid golf buddy, and I am working with several of his artists, andnot just musicians. He just hooked me up with that hot new comedian out of the Bronx. Not to mention I am now his personal attorney."

"Richard, that's great! Congratulations," Maggie said as she reached out and touched his arm.

"Thank you, Maggie," he responded as he put his hand over hers. "I never realized how much of a godsend you were to me until you left. Not just in matters of business. I really miss you."

Maggie slowly slipped her hand from under his, and sat back in her chair. "Man, when it rains, it pours," she said softly.

"Sorry?"

"Nothing."

"Well, anyway, when your dad extended the invite, I confess I was hesitant. You and I ended things rather bitterly." Maggie attempted to speak; Richard held up his hand to stop her. "Yes, I know, I was the one. But since this is a time of family and good feelings, I thought now would be a time to, I don't know…" his hand reached out for hers again. "…extend an olive branch and see if we could, at the very least, get together every once in a while?"

The laugh that emitted from Maggie's mouth was loud enough to surprise even her. "You're joking, right?"

Richard was shocked. "No, Maggie. I'm not. I thought your father's phone call was like a sign from God or something."

"Oh Richard. Please, don't be offended, but being apart has been really good for me. And while I'd like to be in a relationship, well, I just think that you and I getting together would be…"

Richard leaned forward as Maggie searched for the appropriate words.

"…an emotional and spiritual step backward for both of us, don't you think?"

This was not the answer that he expected. He figured

that their time apart, coupled with the fact that she was still single, would have been enough to bring this woman back to her senses. It would have worked with any other woman.

"Perhaps you're right," he said, wiping his mouth with a napkin. "Life goes on, right?"

Maggie was relieved. "But I do appreciate the offer. Let's just enjoy the evening. Everything's been so great."

Matty tapped Maggie on the shoulder. "Aunt Maggie? Can you help me and M&M with this puzzle we started?"

That was all the opportunity she needed to release her from the awkwardness her honestly had brought to light. "Sure, baby. Give me a sec. I'll meet you in the other room. Excuse me, Richard."

Once again, Richard couldn't help but focus on the fact that it was a Buchanan who came between him and Maggie, completely messing up the order of his life. He was angered beyond words. "Sure," he said with the sweetest of smiles. "Like I said, it's the season of family." Maggie rose cheerfully from her chair and took Matty's hand as he led the way. Richard's smile immediately faded to a more rueful expression.

"But they ain't *your* family, no matter how many puzzles you fix," he said bitterly under his breath.

Joe stood in the hallway that led to the family room. His body language communicated that he was watching the twins in the den; but it was actually the best place for him to stand in order for him to hear whatever he could from Maggie's conversation with Richard.

"Did you catch all that?" she asked as she passed by.

He stared down into the drink he'd been nursing. "I have no idea what on earth you're talking about," he said.

They never made eye contact, but she could feel a

sense of relief that practically radiated from him.

When Richard had finished his dinner, the rest of the family assembled for dessert. Maggie had trouble deciding between Janice's apple and Elise's chocolate chess pies. Feeling comfortable in her surroundings, she took a taste of both. Neither piece was all that substantial, so she indulged without a hint of self consciousness.

Taking her coffee and dessert into the den, she was met by an astonished Richard. "Whoa," he said as he stared at her plate. "Save some for the rest of us."

For a split second, Maggie didn't know he was speaking to her. "Excuse me?" she said.

"'Tis the season for your diet rules to go out the window?"

"Richard!" said Lenore.

"For real, you've gotta appreciate a woman who isn't afraid to go to town at the dessert table. You go girl with your healthy appetite!"

Hiding her face behind a plate to conceal the laugh she was suppressing, Sissy got up and went into the kitchen. Joe rose from his place with the kids to intervene, but Richard continued his assault.

"I mean, let's face it, it didn't work out, Maggie and me, but I know there is a man out there who loves a woman who does what she can..." he motioned directly and brazenly at her backside, his hands positioned like a director framing a shot, "...to keep that big, soft, voluptuous cushion! Umph!"

# Chapter 32

lright buddy, back off," Joe exclaimed.
"Richard Davidson, *that's enough*!" Lenore shouted. Everyone else was surprised, incensed and confused all at once. They had seen the two of them chatting amiably just minutes before. The origin of his cruelty was a mystery to everyone except for Maggie.

One thing was certain; the man was smooth; smooth enough to dupe her father and to endear himself to the Hammonds; smooth enough to lead her to believe that the two could peacefully coexist.

It was all part of his twisted game. And she was certain it was the only reason he accepted her father's invitation. Normally, Maggie was able to deflect his bullets, but today he'd successfully lulled her into a place of false security. When she didn't give him his way, he decided to hit her where it hurt most. It might have been a childish move, but he played her like the Steinway in the living room - and she fell for every single, suavely-nuanced note.

Exposure and vulnerability covered her as she looked down at the confections on her plate. They might as well have been made of dirt and stone. They no longer appealed to her.

A chill settled around the room as no one quite knew what to say.

Richard rose from his seat, straightened his tie and

with the finesse of a stealth assassin, gave his hosts a nod and maneuvered his way toward the front door. "I should get going," he said. "Got an early day at the gym tomorrow."

Facing a furious Joe while keeping Maggie in his periphery, Richard said with a brilliant smile as he ran his hands across the front of his suit jacket, "It's gonna take a couple of sessions to work this fabulous dinner off. Maggie, you shouldn't have canceled that membership, or I'd ask you to come with me. We used to have some great workouts together…when you were able to keep up, that is."

Janice's hand rose to cover her open mouth. Even from the kitchen, Sissy began to feel the extremism in Richard's words. "Geez," she said to herself as she sipped her coffee. "This is kinda brutal. Wonder what Maggie did to deserve this?"

"Son, I think Mrs. West is right; that's more than enough," said Matthew, who cast a sideways glance at Dexter. Horrified, Dexter ushered Richard out of the room. Before exiting, he turned for a final time and wished everyone a happy Thanksgiving.

With the attention squared on Richard's departure, Maggie left her plate on the coffee table in the den and retreated to the upstairs guest room to pull herself together.

The ride back to Maggie's house was as silent as the grave. Lenore sat in the back seat, praying that Dexter wouldn't add insult to injury by saying something in Richard's defense. But knowing him as she did, she could feel the storm coming over the horizon in the form of the words that were preparing to escape her husband's mouth. Before Lenore could stop him, he broke the quiet with the worst possible question:

"Did you have to take *two* pieces of pie?"

Maggie nearly slammed on the brakes, as Lenore buried her head in her hands.

"Daddy!" Maggie cried out.

Lenore reached up and firmly grabbed her husband's shoulder, ceasing any further attempt at conversation.

"Maggie, baby…what are you still doing up?"

Elegant even in a robe and hair rollers, Lenore West made her way down the steps to sit with her daughter in her living room. Maggie was in her favorite spot, curled up with a throw pillow, staring out the window.

"I couldn't sleep," she said as her mother sat down next to her.

"Well, we can chalk this up as being one of our more lively holidays, couldn't we?" she asked as the two women laughed.

"No doubt."

"Maggie, I can't speak for Richard. But as far as your father is concerned, it's his desire to see you settled and happy above and beyond everything else."

"But he doesn't *get* it. He's never gotten it. I *want* to be settled. I *want* to be happy. What I *don't* want is that life with Richard. I don't care how perfect it looks on paper. The man is just wrong for me."

"Well, after tonight, I think he gets it. Amazing how your father can be a paragon of intelligence when he puts that judge's robe on, but when it comes to the day to day affairs of his own household…"

"I know, right?" Maggie said as they laughed again. Lenore reached over and gave Maggie a hug.

"Give him time, baby. Now that he's hip to the whole thing with Richard, I think things will get better."

"I know. It's not so bad. I know he means well; I just wish he wasn't so…"

"That's why I'm here. You know that line from that movie - he might be the head of this house, but I'm the neck, and can move him any way I want."

Maggie laughed softly. "Thanks mom. I love you. And I love being your daughter."

"You make it easy, baby," said Lenore. "I couldn't be prouder to be your mother."

# Chapter 33

Maggie stood in a Wal-Mart checkout line, perusing an article in a country music magazine. It had a feature on Deana and Charles in their Hendersonville, Tennessee home; celebrating their life both personally and professionally as one of the true "power couples" in entertainment. Beaming from beneath her fiery mane of impossibly healthy hair, Deana radiated an innate beauty that was the stuff of legend. She even gave tips on how to maintain that natural glow she possessed by way of a simple regimen of soap and water to cleanse the skin, olive oil to moisturize, drinking water regularly, a healthy organic diet and long walks for exercise.

Maggie couldn't help but smile. While nearly all of Deana's claims were true, Maggie could recall on more than one occasion having tagged along as their road manager took midnight trips for a double-decker cheeseburger with the works. Other times it might be an order of deep fried hot wings. Whatever the case, there was always an occasion where Deana would acquire a tour-time yen for something truly fattening that would be consumed behind closed doors.

There were tour pictures as well-snapshots of Deana in concert. Maggie winced as she saw her own image in one of the photos. In reality, it wasn't a horrible picture of

Maggie. But the angle from which the photographer had shot did little in her eyes to minimize… what did Richard call it?

*That soft, voluptuous cushion…*

Quickly shutting the magazine, Maggie closed her eyes and groaned softly, suddenly planning an exit strategy from the line, back to where the diet pills were sold.

"You know, I like her music, but she's nothing without those backup singers she's got," said a voice over Maggie's shoulder.

The sound gave Maggie a jolt as she turned around and saw Joe behind her in the checkout line.

Several days had passed since the events of Thanksgiving; a night made slightly less painful by Maggie spending some healing time with her parents before they joined the Hammonds for the ride back to Ohio.

Suddenly running into Joe at that moment had unearthed that awkward feeling in Maggie once again. Not just for herself, but for everyone who was there to witness Richard's antics that night.

"Hey jumpy," Joe said smiling broadly. "What brings you to our friendly neighborhood Wal-Mart?"

Maggie gestured to the cleaning products in her cart. "I've got some straightening up to do after Hurricane Dexter," she said. "Daddy fixed some stuff around my house. He's great at home repair, but leaves disaster in his wake when he does it. What are you up to?"

"I'm just coming home from work. Thought I'd pick up some stuff for a science project Gwennie's putting together for school," he said, holding up his shopping bag. "I was actually going to call you tonight and check on how you were doing."

They both knew this line of conversation was silly and

safe. But something needed to be said; so Maggie decided to take the first step in addressing it. "Listen Joe, I'm so sorry that your house became the setting for my personal soap opera. I hope we didn't ruin your Thanksgiving."

Joe's smile faded to one of a more thoughtful expression. "I'm sorry you had to go through it at all. But don't worry about where it happened." He stopped for a moment and let out a chuckle.

"What?" Maggie asked.

"All I could think was how Grace wouldn't have stood for it." Joe said, his laughter growing stronger.

"You think she would have cussed Richard out?"

Joe gave Maggie an incredulous look. "That would have been just for starters. She wouldn't have given a thought to her parents, your parents, common decency…"

The two of them continued to laugh at the thought as Maggie placed her items on the conveyor belt. The safety of the moment led her to practically blurt out the question, "Would you like to go for coffee sometime?"

Without a moment's hesitation he said cheerfully, "I'd love it. But I've got a better idea. Excuse me for a second. I'm gonna make a call."

Sissy was pulling leftovers out of Joe's refrigerator to prepare dinner when his phone rang. Feeling like the mistress of the manor, she smiled as she dodged the twins racing through the kitchen before answering brightly, "Buchanan residence."

"Hey Sis, it's Joe."

"Joey! Hi there…when are you getting home? I'm just heating some stuff up for dinner."

"Sis, have I ever told you what an angel you are? Dinner is the very reason I'm calling."

Sissy stopped in the center of the kitchen, unsure of

what to do. "Oh, were you thinking about something else? I was gonna try and do something with this leftover turkey. But if you want to go out, I can have the kids ready in no time flat…"

"Whoa, whoa, whoa, slow down, hon. I was going to ask if you wouldn't mind hanging out for a few more hours and make sure the kids get something to eat."

"Oh," she said, crestfallen. "Is everything okay? Are you stuck at the University?"

"Not exactly," he said. "You see, I ran into Maggie at Wal-Mart…"

Despite her deepening disappointment, Sissy maintained composure. "Really? Tell her hi."

"I will. And you know, after all that craziness last week, I think she needs someone to talk to. It got me thinking that this is usually something Grace would do, but…I'd like to take her out for a nice dinner."

The words echoed in Sissy's head as her irritation with Maggie West began to simmer once again. Joe couldn't hear her throw the dish towel across the room; he did, however, hear the faux charm in her voice as she said, "What a great friend you are! Go, do your thing, and have a great time. I've got the fort held down here. Again, tell Maggie I said hi."

"I sure will. And I'll say it one more time - you are an angel! We won't be out too late."

"Okay, Bye!" Sissy put the receiver down, as Gwen came into the kitchen and picked up the discarded dishtowel. "Looks like it's just us, for dinner tonight, kiddo," Sissy said. "Your dad and Maggie are gonna go out for a bite to eat."

Oblivious to the subtext, Gwen responded with a cheerful, "Oh, cool. You need some help, Aunt Sissy??

                                      

Sissy nodded with a smile. As Gwen turned on some music, the two of them busied themselves with dinner.

# Chapter 34

Joe and Maggie settled on a trendy Asian bistro that was frequented by celebrity and civilian alike. The place had a warm, dimly lit atmosphere that put the two of them instantly at ease.

Huddled around the mini lamp in the center of the table, their eyes had barely begun to adjust to the print on their menus when Maggie heard someone call her name.

"Deana, Hi!"

"Hi there, honey!" Deana responded. Her eyes clearly focused on Joe, her tone practically begging for an introduction, she said, "Well, well…looks like someone's out on the town tonight. Who's your friend?"

"Deana, this is Joe Buchanan. Joe, The Boss Lady."

"This is a real thrill," Joe said as he rose from his side of the booth. "My daughter Gwen is a huge fan. In fact, our whole family is."

A look of realization covered Deana's face. "Oh, okay. You're…"

"Yes, this is my best friend's…Grace's, um…" Maggie said, unable to finish the sentence.

"Well, it's a real thrill to meet *you*," Deana said as she gave him an impulsive and extremely firm embrace.

The hug caught him slightly off guard. "Oh…hey…okay. Alrighty then…aaaand we're hugging," he said nervously. Maggie put a clenched fist to her mouth, not wanting to laugh out loud.

With absolutely no clue as to how deeply she'd invaded Joe's personal space, Deana finally pushed him out to arm's length, never letting go of his shoulders. "Maggie has always spoken of your family so warmly. It broke my heart to hear about your sweet wife."

"I turn my back to pay the bill, and I find my wife's cozying up to another guy," said Charles.

"I think my friend needs to be rescued," Maggie joked. "Charles Timmons, this is Joe Buchanan."

"I'll explain later," Deana said out of the side of her mouth as if she were harboring some state secret.

"I'm sure you will, Dee. Joe, it's a pleasure to meet you," Charles said, shaking Joe's hand.

Just then, a small child captured Deana's attention by way of a pat on the leg. As if someone had flipped a switch, she turned on her megawatt smile and knelt down to the boy's level, chatting cheerfully, even reaching up to smooth his hair. The parents of the adorable tot stood just a few feet away, gushing from afar as the child obtained an autograph from their favorite singer.

Motioning for the parents to come closer, she engaged in conversation with them, before agreeing to pose for a photograph. "Maggie," she said, "Get in here for this. You guys have just got to meet one of my backup singers. Maggie, these are the, um, Adamses, and they're here in Nashville all the way from Columbus, Ohio. Maggie, aren't you from around there?"

Maggie graciously nodded, then looked to Charles who returned her glance with his own knowing smile. It was what The Boss Lady did best: Her accessibility was a major part of her appeal.

Joe offered to take the photo and gathered the whole

group around an empty table. The family gave their thanks and appreciation, phoning family and friends even before they reached the front door.

Returning to their booth after saying their good byes to Deana and Charles, Joe and Maggie sat quietly for a few moments. Finally, Joe spoke:

"Holy crap. That made me dizzy!"

Maggie laughed out loud. Joe continued. "Seriously, I am worn out…and you can *not* judge a book by its cover." He tried rubbing his shoulder where Deana's hand had been. "That woman might be small, but she's like that doll with the Kung-Fu grip."

Maggie wiped a tear from her eye as she continued to laugh. "Welcome to the music industry in Nashville."

"How can a person live like that?"

"Well, Deana's used to it. It's been her M.O. for the past decade. It's part of living life as a high profile celebrity."

"That's how it works then?" he asked.

"Yep, I guess so."

Joe shook his head and took a sip from his water glass. "It's funny, but usually, when I think of talent to celebrate, I think of you."

"Really? Nah, I'm not a star, Joe. Now Deana; she's…"

"She's an entertainer; a personality. And I think there's a difference."

Maggie was confused. "I'm not sure I follow."

"Well, don't get me wrong, she's good at what she does. And she can certainly captivate when she's got an audience. She's a physically stunning woman, but she's mostly show. Sure, she can sing, but when I hear *you*, it's as if I'm on this fantastic four minute journey. You're telling a story that you've written, from your heart, all wrapped up in that amazing voice."

Maggie was warmed by Joe's words. "What I get when

I'm around Deana is that she needs to whip people up in a frenzy in order to get them drawn in," he said. "You do it just by being you. Your elegance, your presence, the way you radiate…then, you hit 'em with those pipes of yours."

Maggie found herself unsure of what to say. But Joe's assessment of her talent and his ardent belief in her was overwhelming. She stared down at her menu, afraid that if she rose to meet his gaze, she might cry.

"Hey," Joe said, sliding his hand across the table to slip his fingers through hers. "I mean it. You, to me, are the true star. It's only a matter of time until someone more important than Deana and Charles recognizes it without being intimidated by it."

"Intimidated?"

"Absolutely," he said. "Correct me if I'm wrong, but this is my theory: It seems to me that Richard, your father, and the Timmonses all see your talent, and it scares the heck out of them. The reasons might be different, but the reaction is the same."

What Joe was saying surprised her a bit, but as she began to process, none of it seemed too far fetched.

"That's why they treat you the way they do. If they weren't so scared that you'd eclipse them, they'd be doing whatever they could to help you fly; not hold you down with harsh words and bullying."

"I think my dad cares," said Maggie. "But I also think the music business seems like an uncertain little playground to him. He doesn't see what I do as a real job yet."

Joe was astonished. "You've been making a living at it for over twenty years! What's it gonna take for him to get it?"

"A record deal. A Grammy. A world tour of my own. I dunno. And now that I'm the age I am…"

"You know what my mother told me once? *The day it's too late is the day you're dead.* Don't worry about how old you are. You might not be a teeny bopper pop star…"

Maggie chuckled at his verbiage, but continued to listen.

"…but you're every bit as good as any one of those half-dressed-little-whatevers in those videos. And that's what scares them all. Not that you'll fail. But that you'll succeed. You'll soar! And you'll do it without their help. And if I might be so bold…"

"Could I stop you?"

"No…I think the fact that you wear your insecurity and self doubt so closely to the surface is all the ammo they need to keep you dragging the bottom."

Maggie sat back in her chair, nonplussed. Nobody, not even Grace, was able to articulate her heart as accurately as Joe had done. Joe got it. And that scared her. She quickly drew her hand back and grabbed her own glass of water.

"You know? I was hoping to work with M&M on her piano lessons this week. Is she still a little behind?" A quick sip was taken to hide the emotions she didn't want to convey.

Joe picked up her signal and allowed her to change the subject. But that feeling he had in the kitchen on Thanksgiving had returned with a vengeance and started to spin around in his chest. This woman was doing insane things to his heart.

He moved in closer, resting his elbows on the table.

"Yeah, she is a little. Stop by any time before her lesson on Tuesday. I'm sure she'll appreciate it," he said with a smile.

They confined their talk to safe subjects for the rest of the meal, and the evening passed by quite comfortably.

Joe wouldn't allow her to pick up the check when it came. "I'll take you up on that offer for coffee, if you're still game?"

"I didn't mean tonight, silly," she said. Sensing his disappointment, she quickly added, "But since there's a Starbucks a couple of doors down…"

"The one at Five Points usually isn't as busy this time of night," he said.

An hour into their coffee, they both noticed the staff had been stacking chairs on tables and wiping things down.

"Guess it's time to go," he said.

"Yeah," Maggie replied. "You, kind sir, are the king of the impromptu evening. Thank you."

"You're welcome. Come on, I'll take you to your car."

Just then, Joe's cell phone began to ring.

# Chapter 35

Hello? Oh, hey Sis. Yeah, I'm fine. We just got deep into a conversation, and lost track of time. Sorry to keep you waiting."

"Oh, it's okay," she said meekly, knowing she probably sounded a little too obvious. "I hadn't heard from you in a while, and I was just checking to see if you were alright. Oh, and Gwen said something about you picking up some stuff so she could do her science project…?"

"Ahhh," he said putting the heel of his hand to his forehead. "I totally forgot. I'm on my way back."

"Excellent. The twins are in bed, just so you know."

"Well, if you're tired, which, after an evening with those little people, I'm sure you are, just sack out in the guest room and head home tomorrow."

Sissy was thrilled. "Well, now that you mention it, they did give me a run for my money. Thanks, Joe."

"Of course hon. It's the least that I can do. Make yourself at home, and I'll get there soon."

"Alright, Joe. You be safe now. See you when you get home."

Sissy hung up the phone and finished picking up around the downstairs area. After sending Gwen upstairs to her room to wind down her day, then checking on the twins, she tiptoed across the hall to the master bedroom.

The moon was streaming in through the double doors that led to a private outdoor patio, so there was little need for her to turn on the light.

Sissy took her time and inspected every inch of the room; the sleekly finished dresser drawers, the back of the chaise lounge, the end of the king sized bed. She stepped briefly into the master bath - the air was still thick with the scent of Joe's soap.

There was a bath towel folded over the shower curtain rod, most likely used that morning when Joe was getting ready. Sissy buried her face in the towel, enveloping herself in the scent. She did the same thing when she removed one of his older sweatshirts folded in the closet-grey, with the University logo barely visible on the front, and a neckline that was showing signs of wear and tear.

Stripping down to her underwear, she felt something delicious about her level of undress in this room. She donned Joe's sweatshirt, her long shapely legs practically flowing beneath the hem. She studied herself in the full length mirror on the wall; turning this way and that, gently tossing her hair, pleased with how alluring she looked.

As she heard the approach of Joe's car, she quickly picked up her clothes, and made her way upstairs to the guest room.

There were no thoughts of her baby sister's previous occupation here. At this point, Joe was Sissy's goal. She would not be deterred or denied. Whatever his current fascination with Maggie West, it was time for Sissy to do whatever she could set her own personal wheels in motion in order to get him shift his focus to her.

# About the Author

With a resume that includes appearances at Carnegie Hall, The House of Blues in Chicago, the Grand Ol' Opry, five European and three Australian concert tours, Marcia Ware's musical background is as varied as it is colorful. In addition to her own celebrated solo work, she has provided background vocals for such artists as Lorrie Morgan, Pam Tillis, Peter Frampton, Mary Wilson of the Supremes, Gospel greats Bill and Gloria Gaither and the legendary Chaka Khan. She has also been a featured vocalist with the famed Funk Brothers of Motown.

An aspiring actress, she has appeared in several episodes of the ABC drama, *Nashville,* playing…surprise, surprise…a background singer.

Marcia counts first among her many passions her relationship with her Savior, time spent with her family and her amazing boyfriend, songwriting, travel, harmonizing with the radio, good food, endless games of Candy Crush on her Smartphone, Daniel Day-Lewis movies and Ohio State Buckeyes football.

She resides in Franklin, TN.

*And now...a sneak peek at*

# Maggie's Refrain

Joe felt the same nervous knots in his own stomach as he made his way down the corridor to the room where Maggie was working. For the longest time he'd sat in his car, wrestling for hours as to whether or not he should go inside. But as he looked down at the gorgeous chain on his wrist, he knew that there was no way he couldn't be there. He couldn't let her leave town without at the very least confronting the situation that lay before them.

On the one hand, he was scared that Sissy was right - that it was too soon after Grace's death for him to get into some *big emotional thing*. Maybe this would be too much for the families to take: the Hammonds seeing their daughter being replaced...by her best friend, of all people. Sure, the children loved her, but to see her in any role other than *Aunt Maggie*? He was acutely aware of the fact that they might not be able to get their young minds around it.

On the other hand, for the first time since Grace's death, Joe couldn't escape the fact that he was starting to feel an intense healing, and there was no denying Maggie's presence played an enormous role in that. For the first time in a long while, he felt a sense of virility and vitality that he thought had been buried with his wife. Maybe it was too soon to call it love; but maybe it was just the right time to find out exactly what it was. Maybe...

He followed the music down a narrow hallway then down some stairs to a large, dimly lit room that was dominated by a massive sound board. Tweaking knobs and subtly adjusting levers, Charles turned from his work to acknowledge Joe's entrance and shake his hand. He offered Joe an available chair in a back corner as he whispered, "We're just about done; you almost missed it."

Joe smiled and nodded as he took his seat. There were several others in the room, including a man who sat next to Charles at the board. Periodically, the two would lean their heads toward one another to converse, but everyone else in the room was silent.

On the other side of an enormous window that stretched from floor to ceiling, Joe saw three men and three women, including Maggie. They stood in groups of two in front of three separate microphones. Some had headphones covering both ears, some had one ear covered and the other exposed. They sat on stools or stood on tattered Oriental rugs that spread over hardwood floors.

Rich, thick fabric that served both acoustic and aesthetic purpose hung from sections of the colorful walls and vaulted ceiling. Antique wrought-iron candelabras stood in various parts of the room to provide ambiance.

The singers' harmonies were glorious as they wrapped around Deana's simple scratch vocals. Joe marveled at how the engineers could simply push a button and in a moment's time, anything that might have been sung incorrectly was erased in a seamless transition. He was amazed at how they could perform the same passages over and over again in order to create the sound of a choir three times their size.

Caught up in the shared excitement in the control room, Joe found himself smiling broadly and nearly applauded at the song's triumphant conclusion.

"Alright guys and gals, that was fantastic," said Charles. "That's gonna do it for everybody but Maggie. I want to do some quick ad-libs on this last song."

The other singers exited the room and left Maggie alone at her mic. "Okay, hon," said Charles, "I don't need to tell you a thing. We're gonna roll the track, and you just do what you do."

The music began, and Maggie closed her eyes. Five seconds into her take, Maggie was able to cast off any constraints of tension she might have felt. She was home, completely in her element. As the sounds emerged, whole and full from her throat, the entire room unleashed a cacophony of sounds that signified the one fact that was never in doubt: Maggie was a true phenomenon.

Placing embellishments wherever she felt appropriate, building from soft, yet passionate tones to huge, gospel-infused bombast, the ride that Joe once described as Maggie's voice was taking everyone in that room to heights and depths that left everyone virtually breathless.

Joe watched as she commandeered the journey. His heart warmed not only by what he was hearing, but also by the beautiful vessel from which it came, Joe felt a sudden rush of inspiration.

Quietly making his way back to the hallway, he asked an abundantly tattooed young man where he could find Darla Dayton. The kid pointed behind him to the smaller of two women leaning against the wall engaged in light conversation.

"Darla," he asked.

She was willing to bet her next paycheck that this handsome guy standing in front of her was the cause of Maggie's distraction. "Yeah," she said with a smile. "You're Joe, aren't you?"

Joe was afraid of any negative conversation that might have concerned him. "Yes, I am," he said sheepishly.

"Don't get your knickers in a twist, all I know is good stuff about you," she said with a wink. Joe blushed.

"And there's no need to worry, girlfriend's had her poker face on for the most part all day," she said. "But I'm not gonna lie - she's been a bit diverted. Said something about having the best and worst night of her life last night." Her inflection of the end of that phrase went upwards, as if she was hoping to glean some information from him.

Joe smiled and said, "Well, I don't, um…*date*-and tell." He punctuated his sentence with a wink of his own.

"You're a stinker. I like that in a man."

Joe laughed at the flirtatious moxie of the petite blonde. "I know you're taking Maggie to the airport today, but I was wondering if I could talk to you about surprising her at the airport when she gets back."

Darla was touched. Particularly in light of the slight despair she'd seen in Maggie's eyes. "I think she'd love that," she said with genuine graciousness. "I'll not say a word."

Just then, a muffled round of cheers could be heard from within the control room. The door opened, and people exited. "Girl, you are the Queen of the one-take! Good Job, honey," Charles said.

"Guess they're done," said Joe.

"She's got a few minutes before we have to head out," said Darla. She handed him a slip of paper. "Here's her return flight info. Go talk to her. I know she'd love to see you."

"Thanks Darla. It was nice to meet you."

"You too, sugar." As he walked away, she looked at the woman standing next to her with whom she'd been chatting. Both of them offered low whistles of appreciation.

Joe waded through a sea of individuals to make his way back to Maggie. He stopped at the doorway and saw her chatting amiably with a striking African-American man. Joe couldn't tell what they were saying, but if he went only by body language, it would seem that they had a very familiar level of comfort with one another. The young man touched her face, and she reached up to touch the back of his hand.

As she caught sight of Joe, he felt his own initial fears and ambivalence return. He managed a smile and strode across the room confidently. "You were amazing, Mags," he said.

Maggie felt a rush of excitement shoot through every corner of her body as she reached out to take his hand. "I want you to meet Jared Fox," she said. "Jared, this is Joe Buchanan."

Jared's smile immediately illuminated the features on his boyish brown face. "Very nice to meet you," he said with a strong baritone. "Maggie, I'll talk to you later. Are we still on for dinner when you get back?"

"Absolutely. Merry Christmas."

"Merry Christmas. To both of you," he said as he answered his ringing cell phone.

Joe gave Jared a polite nod.

After saying good bye to Charles and acknowledging the compliments of the other musicians as they passed by, Joe and Maggie made their way out to Darla's car.

"I wonder where she is," said Maggie, looking around. "Oh well, she knows what time we have to leave. Did you enjoy yourself today? How much of it did you see?"

Joe hair was instantly flipped away from his face as he stood in the direction of the wind. He was no longer able to hide the mounting disappointment he was feeling and his expression began to darken. "I caught the last song, and that deal you did at the end. Like I said, you were absolutely awesome."

Maggie noticed the shift. "Thanks," she said tentatively. "What's wrong?"

Joe stared down at the ground and shifted his weight from foot to foot, partly due to the chill that the wind had brought, and partly from nervous apprehension.

"Maggie," he began.

Maggie's heart began to sink. It was an all too familiar tone, a tone that for her had always preceded a supreme letdown.

It was the tone a 13 year old Jimmy Steinmetz used right before he discouraged her in his gauche teenage way from having a crush on him because he thought she was fat and ugly.

It was the tone that three different gospel labels had used right before they told her how great she sounded, but felt that she didn't have the image to promote a successful singing career.

It was the tone Charles had used when she told him she still had dreams of branching out on her own.

Bracing herself once again, she immediately noticed how much more adept she was at handling the moment the older she became. Perhaps by this point, she was simply numb.

She looked him squarely in the eye. "Yes, Joe?" she said without an ounce of weakness.

Joe felt himself losing ground, and struggled to rally. He said her name again. "Maggie…"

Maggie folded her arms and raised an eyebrow, daring him to go on. His cowardice won…for the moment.

"I just wanted to say, thank you for this," he said, showing her that he was wearing her gift.

She softened briefly. "That goes both ways. I loved

what you gave me. I didn't think it was appropriate to wear to a recording session though…"

They were both relieved that they were able to laugh, even if only for a second. But the wall in Joe's mind was still high, so he chose to stay his course.

"Listen, about last night…"

"It shouldn't have happened," Maggie said, cutting him off. Better for her to administer the initial blow; she found that it hurt less that way. "It was a huge mistake. I mean, what were we thinking?"

"Mag, I don't know what's happening with me," he said. "I do know you mean the world to me…"

"But…"

"That's just it; I don't know how to fill in that blank. I mean, I think I do. When I'm by myself, I can come up with six ways til Sunday as to why we shouldn't get involved. Why I'm not ready to take that step…but then I see you…"

"Maggie, we need to get going in about 5-10 minutes," Darla called from the main door of the studio.

"Okay," she replied, turning her attention back to Joe.

He picked up where he left off. "Then I see you…and it's like, everything just goes out the window." He leaned in closer to her just as her perfume wafted his way.

"I understand," she said softly.

Joe shoved his hands in the pockets of his jeans. He was afraid that if he touched her, even put his fingertips against hers, it would all be over with no going back. He continued to speak from his fear.

"I just don't wanna hold you back, Maggie."

"Hold me back? How would you…"

"You've got so much ahead of you. I know that this is just a stepping stone for you. You should be with someone who can help you celebrate who you are and what you do so well."

Maggie was genuinely confused. "Joe, what are you talking about?"

"You're young. You're on the road. You need someone with whom you've got more in common." He pointed in the direction of the building. "What about that guy you were talking to a few minutes ago. Jake?"

It took Maggie a few seconds but then it dawned on her. "No, Jared. What about him?"

"Yeah, Jared. He's good looking; you guys are in the same profession…"

Maggie held up her hand to stop him. 'Hold up," she said. Shaking her head as if that action will help her make sense of what Joe was insinuating, she said again, "Jared?"

Joe wondered if he was doomed to open his mouth only to change feet when it came to expressing himself to a woman. "I saw the two of you talking, it looked fairly intimate…"

"Jared?!"

"Yeah, I think we covered that…"

"Joe, I…I…don't know how to even respond to that. Do you really think…"

Maggie scoffed again as Joe attempted to protest. "Do I think what, Maggie?"

"I have to go, Joe. Merry Christmas."

"No!" he said as he gently grabbed her hand. "Do I think what?"

Maggie wanted to walk away. In truth, she wanted to run. But she wasn't going to let him off the hook with a simple dramatic exit. She turned to face him.

"Joe, *think* about what you've just implied…in light of what happened last night."

His face softened with immediate understanding. How could he have been so shallow to think that Maggie would connect with him so passionately in one moment, only to offer her affection to someone else not even twenty-four hours later? He knew that he was merely cultivating excuses for not getting close to her. He felt embarrassed and childish.

Just then, Darla came to the car. "Maggie," she said. "We should get going."

The tension between Maggie and Joe was obvious, forcing Darla to waste no time in getting behind the wheel and closing the door to offer them a few final seconds of privacy.

"Maggie," Joe finally said. "I'm sorry. Really, I am."

Maggie then said something that she would, for the rest of her days regret. She showed Joe no mercy as she sliced into him with her final comment. Her eyes narrowed as she practically hissed: "You're right Joe. From where I stand, you're about as sorry as it gets."

His hurt was visible immediately. Maggie turned away and got into the car, primarily because she couldn't believe how quickly she lashed out simply to wound him. It was something Richard would have done, and it disgusted her.

As he had done in his driveway just one night before, Joe stood in the parking lot and watched helplessly as another car took Maggie away.

Jared jogged over to Joe, a look of disappointment on his face. "Oh man, did Maggie just leave?" he asked.

"Um, yeah," Joe said with a heavy heart. Jared motioned to a tall, sturdy woman with a deep complexion. She had a quiet beauty and uncomplicated sense of dress.

"Dang," said Jared. "My fiancée just showed up, and I wanted her to meet Maggie."

Joe blinked and recovered from his daydream state. "Fiancée?"

Jared glowed as the woman joined him and took his hand. "Yeah, Maggie's gonna sing at our wedding in the spring, and we were gonna take her out to dinner when she got back so we could go over the songs, and thank her in advance."

"She singing at your wedding," he said, slightly stunned.

"Uh huh," replied Jared. "I was hoping to catch her before she went to the airport so they could at least meet ahead of time. I'm sorry; I've forgotten your name. Joe, was it?"

"Yes, I'm Joe."

"Well Joe, meet the love of my life, Diana."

"Diana, like the huntress," Joe replied, extending his hand. Diana gracefully offered hers as they shook.

"Exactly," she said with a bright smile. "I hunted this one down for sure!"

Joe hid his embarrassment by laughing along with the couple. Completely floored, Joe set his gaze in the direction of the car and sighed. "Well," he said as he fumbled with his car keys, "It was great meeting both of you."

"You too," Jared responded. "I don't know how long you've been friends with her, but Maggie has been like a big sister to me since I moved here three years ago. She heard me sing at a showcase, and kinda took me under her wing. Got me connected with some cool friends of hers. Now I'm getting ready to sign my own deal. She even co wrote a couple of songs with me; didn't charge a thing. She's amazing, isn't she?"

Joe found it difficult to breathe; it was as if someone has set a boulder on his chest. Somehow, he managed to say, "Amazing doesn't even begin to cover it."